LOVING CALEB

LOVING CALEB

When Love is Denied From the Start

SANDREKA Y. BROWN

SEEBOOKZ PUBLISHING LLC

LAGRANGE GEORGIA

iSeebookz Publishing LLC
Suite 137B Commerce Ave #300
Lagrange Georgia 30241

ISBN 979-8-9854863-6-0

Editor: Y. D. Rowland
Interior Design: Publishing Services
Cover Design: iSeebookz Publishing Graphic designer
Front cover: Male Photo: AI generated Adobe Stock images

First Edition 2024

10 9 8 7 6 5 4 3 2 1

Author Publications

Romance Publications by the Author
Love Bethany
The Birds and The Bees
Gender Related

Professional Self Help Publications
Teacher to Teacher
The Teacher's Keeper
Dear God: A Prayer Journal.

Contents

A YEAR LATER

DEDICATION

To everyone navigating the complexities of love and life: may your hearts be filled to overflowing with love as you pursue your purpose. May God's love heal you and dispel all fear, allowing you to embrace the beauty of love wherever it may come. Remember always that you are deeply loved.

PROLOGUE

He watched her as she pushed the door open to leave the bookstore. He saw her in all her glory, confident and with her head held high. She had found her inner peace. Bethany realized that his issues were no longer hers. He questioned his motives and thought...

They say men don't pray...Sorry, but that is a myth.... I need you God!

Caleb

ECHOES OF LOVE

Whispered in Hindsight

I

CALEB'S STORY

She looked at him with contempt. She wished she had never given birth, and she let him know it. He felt it, and he resented her. His own mother. The one woman who carried him for nine months. The one woman he desperately wanted and needed to show him love, to help heal and fill the void and brokenness within him. But that day would never come.

"What do you want, boy? That is what you are and what you will always be, a boy. Even your father," she paused to think and whispered as if not sure... "Isn't a man."

She stared with a blank look as she continued her thoughts. "Why I bothered to have you. I should've aborted you before you were born. Men ain't shit. Aint bout shit won't ever do shit, and then I had to go and create one. Carry one in this body." Her voice trailed off as she looked at her midsection, rubbed the covers over her stomach area, then snatched her hands away and looked up at her son.

She looked Caleb up and down. "I asked you a question. Why you just standing there? What do you want!?"

He thought about talking to her and dismissed speaking his mind. "Nothing," he said, looking at her in the hospital bed. She had suffered a mild stroke. Stress in any form was forbidden. So, he kept himself from giving her a piece of his mind, respectfully.

"See, just like I thought... You ain't about shit. Never gonna be shit, either. Church or no church. Calling yourself a man of God. I see you. I know you. You sleeping around. I see it all over you."

She pointed her finger at him and did a circle in the air. "Just like your grandfather and your lying, molesting uncles." Shaking her head, she repeated Ain't shit for about a minute. Looked at him and said, "You ain't doing right. I smell it. Sin is sin... I know my sin... Do you know yours? Oh, you know, but hell, you can't see it... you in it."

Caleb stood there saying nothing. After a moment of silence, which Caleb welcomed, he heard her whisper the Lord's prayer, and then she looked him dead in the eyes... As if she could see into his soul.

"What's her name, or rather, what are their names."

Caleb looked at her, shocked and feeling some kind of way like, *I wish she didn't put me in the same bag as all the others.*

Caleb was honestly a good man. He loved his wife and his children. Caleb's mom smiled hard. Pointed her finger and said, "I see you; I know you," she busted out laughing and enjoyed her inner thoughts of mirth watching him become uncomfortable. She was good at calling and saying what she meant. She became quiet as the nursing staff came in to give her the nightly sedative. She prayed to God and cursed at Him, then cried herself to sleep.

Caleb took it all in stride; she was his mother. He watched her sleep for hours. It was the best part of visiting her. It was in these moments that he reflected upon her life. This woman. *Why, God, did you give me this woman for a mother?* When he was old enough to understand, his mother really didn't love him. It hit him to the core. As he grew older, he learned of her secrets through eavesdropping and putting two and two together. Caleb began to hate himself for being a male.

His only peace of mind was watching his father as he grew up, giving this woman all he had. Living the life that most men looked down upon. His father was faithful even though he was accused of cheating. He was loving while being labeled as a pimp looking for something in return. Caleb saw this as a young man and found God.

His father on earth exemplified the actions of Christ on earth with this woman, his mother... She didn't deserve her earlier life, and it tainted her. He respected his dad. Both of his parents made him who he was, and in some cases, it scared him and tore him apart on the inside.

His father walked into the room. Caleb, putting his fingers to his lips, motioned to be quiet. Mr. Mitchell nodded and placed his bouquet of flowers on the side table, walked over to his wife, leaned over, and gave her a brief brush of a kiss on her forehead. He didn't want to disturb her peace.

Caleb watched his father lovingly look at this woman who cursed him since the day he was born. Being loved by a man who deserved so much more than what he got by loving her. Did his mother know she got it good? Does his father know it could have been better with a different woman?

His father looked at him concerned. Caleb pointed to the door, and they walked out of her room and into the hospital corridor. Mr. Mitchell understood how his wife could be.

"How you holding up Caleb? How was she today?"

Caleb looked at him, trying to control his emotions, but he was crying inside. "Nothing out of the usual Dad."

Mr. Mitchell looked at him with a knowing look. Like that ain't going to fly with me.

Caleb smiled. Shaking his head. "Ok Ok Ok..." Looking at his dad, the smile faded. He let go of his thoughts of being proper. He was talking to the one person he could tell all without restraint.

"Mom said a lot, and it cut me deep. I don't do any of the things she accuses me of...I may think it. It's like she has a gift to know my fleeting thoughts. It disturbs me 'cause I know her to speak things before they happen. I know she has some type of gift, but no matter how good I do, she still despises me."

Mr. Mitchell nodded. "She is who she is, son. Regardless of life situations or our past that we can't let go of, we owe it to ourselves, to be honest. She doesn't despise you. She is honest. It's hard for her to love, son. But she is a good woman. Broken, but she is good."

Caleb listened and watched his father. He reminisced on family memories, those filled with laughter and joy. He remembered seeing his father light up from seeing his mother laughing so hard she fell off the chair while they talked.

The moments of them two cooking together in the kitchen. These were the moments his father relished. The joy of those moments made married life for his father worthwhile.

She was a mother and wife who cherished, nurtured, and encouraged the family during those times. But it never reached the level of love. It was an acknowledgment that a teacher would give a child or a stranger on the street giving you a compliment for your good behavior. It lasted for a moment, and then it was gone.

Caleb hugged his father, "It's going to be okay, Dad, she will be okay. It was just a mild stroke."

"I know Caleb. She is a fighter. But you got to get home. You been here for hours. Kiss my grandkids for me. Tell them I will be by to see them soon."

Caleb looked at his watch. "You right, Dad, I got to go. Love you. Talk to you later." As he walked away, he heard his father say, "Love you son. Drive safely." Caleb looked back and then waved while saying, "Will do." Caleb left his father at the hospital to spend the night shift with his mother.

Evening traffic was a beast. Caleb thought of home. Looking forward to seeing the kids. It had been a day, and he thought of Tonya. "Call home," he said as he made a left turn and thought of picking up a bottle of wine. He had plans tonight. He missed his wife. She came home a few days ago from a business trip, and since his mother's emergency, they hadn't had time to connect. The speaker system dialed ranged and made the connection.

"Hello."

"Hey, Babe."

"Don't Babe me, Caleb."

Caleb smiled. "I'm driving by Total Wine; you want a bottle of our favorite?"

Calm and cool, she said, "Now, Babe, you know how to get me."

Caleb burst out laughing. "What the kids doing?"

"They running around here getting on my damn nerves. If I hear another request to play Fortnite, I am going to scream. I made them go to the living room and read."

"Did you have a long day working Tonya?"

"It was, even though I was home, and if that's your way of indirectly asking if I fixed dinner? Then the answer is No."

Caleb smiled knowingly. "I'm bringing home dinner; you okay with lasagna, salad, and breadsticks from Scaleni's?"

"You got my favorite dish?"

"Sure did."

"Well then... I'm officially a loved woman."

"See you soon Tonya."

"Caleb, don't hang up. I know you're on the way home, but I have to ask, how is Mama Hazel?"

Caleb dismissed her question. *Tonya really don't care*, he reminded himself inwardly. It was a truth that could not be denied. Although his mother despised him, she truly hated Tonya, and if Hell could open up and swallow his wife whole, his mother would cheer her on the way down. Caleb remained quiet to her question. Tonya waited and then stated.

"We'll talk when you get home."

Caleb heard the click, and the speaker system played the

next song on the station. Caleb hummed the tune as the words flowed in his mind.... *It's been a long time coming, but I know a change...* Turning into the plaza, he turned off the engine. Looking at the store, he checked his account. He was happy to see the zeros at the end of his balance. Work had finally paid off with the last project. This bottle of wine was more than just a connection with Tonya. He hoped she would see him as a real man.

Business and work had not always been lucrative in the past few years. It was wonderful to see his bank account showing a profit. Caleb prayed that God would bless him and keep the flow of business. He walked into the store and selected his bottle of wine. The lady behind the counter smiled at him. Caleb sensed he could have her if he wanted. But he thought of Tonya, made his purchase, and left the store. He thought of his mother and looked back at the cashier with a foreboding feeling.

The cashier smiled at Caleb as he walked away... *man he was fine as hell... If it wasn't for my grad school midterms, I'd pursue that ring or no ring on his finger, which he clearly had.* She turned her attention to the next person in line.

2

TONYA

Tonya watched the clock, checked her missed text messages, and made a phone call. He answered as usual. "Hi!" No greeting was returned, just a question... "He home yet?" The male on the other end asked. "No, he won't be in for another 30 minutes. He went to get wine. What's up, Mike? I saw your text."

"I got to see you tonight, Tonya. You've been gone, and it's been more than two weeks. You know what I need."

"I can't leave tonight, Mike. He hasn't seen me either. I got to handle the home front; you know this." She heard him sigh and then heard the car start. "I am going out tonight, Tonya. Whatever happens, you can't blame a brother. I got needs."

Tonya whined, "C'mon Mike, it's just one more day. Don't do this. Can you give me until midnight? Call me, and I can leave for the office as an excuse. I will come to you. I will, don't do this to me... You know I want out of this marriage."

She heard the engine die and a car door opening and closing. I will give you until midnight, Tonya. If my needs are not met, I will go out. You know I love you, but physically, I am waiting for no one!"

Tonya heard the click as he hung up. Looking at the time, Tonya headed toward the shower. She would be working overtime tonight and was anticipating the second shift more than the first. After her shower, she got out two wine glasses, put on her best lingerie, and waited for Caleb, but traffic was a beast. An accident occurred, causing an hour delay in addition to Caleb's 30-minute commute. Caleb phoned Tonya again to let her know he'd be late and his estimated time of getting home.

Damn, Tonya thought after hanging up. Slipping into a robe, she went to check on the children and heard their groans. Tired of it all, she fixed them sandwiches, made them bathe, and put them to bed early, not hearing their pleas to wait for their father.

Caleb finally pulled up to the Craftsman style, ranch 3 bedroom, 2 bath home. It wasn't small by any means at 1600 square feet, but it was a far cry from the 3200 square foot home Tonya desired. It took both their incomes to support it. Well, mostly Tonya's, as his business income was inconsistent. He was happy that the last four months had shown promise. Another 3 months, and he would be able to make a mortgage payment without Tonya's help or input.

Pushing the automatic garage door opener from his car visor, Caleb drove his 8-year-old Ford Expedition into the garage. He parked it next to Tonya's 4-year-old Mercedes Benz, which she bought with her last bonus check 2 years ago. It was a used car, as Tonya couldn't afford the latest model. But she wouldn't drive anything other than a luxury car. He smiled, happy to know his wife and children drove in style.

Walking into the house, he noticed how quiet it was. Placing the wine into the portable cooler, he went into the kid's rooms and noticed they were sleeping. He missed the opportunity to see them. Looking at his watch, he thought it was strange as he thought about the food he had placed on the kitchen counter. He walked toward the master suite and opened the door only to be greeted by candles and a dimly lit room.

Caleb smiled. Tonya fed into what he wanted by greeting him while on the bed as he turned the corner from the room's entrance. He placed the wine cooler next to the wine glasses and was pleasantly surprised to see Tonya in a black and red baby doll chemise. Caleb was not expecting her to be so enticing. He looked at her in all her glory. Her slim butter pecan complexion glistened in the dim light. Her muscular, toned body was that of a former dancer, and his body responded as he took his fill to look.

Her hair cascaded off to the side across her shoulder, framing her heart-shaped face, which was made up to perfection. His thoughts went inward. He thought of all his pent-up frustrations, and he looked forward to releasing it all with a night of passionate sex; watching her as she walked toward him, he thought... *Damn, she's fine, and she's all mine...*made him forget about his mother and all that he had endured for the day.

Tonya watched him as he looked at her; she saw his hunger

for her, and she worried if she could make this first half of the night end by midnight. Caleb had the look of pulling an all-nighter. *Damn it!* She thought as she walked toward him and smiled all the brighter.

The house alarm showed 1 am as Mike punched in the code to his climate-controlled garage that housed his most-priced cars. Sipping Fou Dre Vodka on ice, he walked into the custom-designed room and thought of Tonya. Mike hated being second in her life after her loser of a husband with no business savvy. He thought of Caleb and his God-fearing ways, and he laughed.

Looking at his cars, which totaled more than 5 million as a whole, he thought of his net worth of 130 million. While that usually got him over his jealousy, it did nothing for his sexual ache for Tonya. She was fine, and she instinctively put her experience to use to treat and appeal to his taste.

I can give her the life she deserves, he thought as...he took a gulp of vodka and winced as it went down his throat. Looking at his watch, Tonya should be here by now... *Damn you, Caleb, she is my woman.* Pulling out his phone, he texted Tonya.

Caleb climaxed for the fourth time, and Tonya was out-done. It had been years since Caleb had made love to her in that manner. Caleb looked at her as he pulled back a wisp of hair behind her ear and kissed her tense-looking forehead.

"What's the matter, Tonya? Are you okay?"

She looked at him and saw a young boy trying to be a man in her eyes, and she smiled, not giving her thoughts away.

"I'm fine, Caleb. I'm just tired. It's been a long week, and after the last four hours..."

Caleb laughed. "I am sorry, but it's just been a lot on my mind. You are a blessing, Tonya."

Tonya said nothing, not wanting to start an intimate conversation, especially not one with God involved. She rolled away from Caleb and got up as her phone binged. She walked to the dresser and looked down at her phone to check her messages. Caleb watched her.

"Don't answer it tonight; I want more of you."

"I got to Caleb; you know how demanding my job is."

Caleb laid back on the bed taking in a full view of her in all her birthday glory, and he showed how much he wanted her. Tonya looked up from her phone at Caleb, his desire showing through the sheets. "Are you serious, Caleb? I'm done; you better go and get a cold shower." She smiled and then looked at her phone one am was the time. She looked at the screen as Project 2 Assistance showed a message. She hated to open it looking at the time. She was late. Caleb walked over to her and kissed her.

"Woman, you better be happy. I love you and think of your well-being... I am off to the showers, unfortunately. You want to join me?"

Tonya laughed. "Boy, that would defeat the purpose of you taking a shower. You on your own."

"Can't knock me for trying." Looking at her hungrily as he walked toward the linen closet in their room to get fresh towels. Tonya swiped over to read the message from Project Assistance 2 (aka Mike) ...

I AM WAITING FOR YOU... DAMN HIM!

Inwardly smiling, she frowned at the message for Caleb's sake... "I have to go in, babe." Caleb looked at her...

"I told you not to look, but what could they possibly want from you at one am Tonya- that can't wait till the morning?"

"You know I took off this week working from home, Caleb; the team is working tonight. I just decided to stay here with you, remember." Caleb questioned the odd hours she kept, and it disturbed him. But she was the stable income for the family. He couldn't complain.

He walked over to her, "Do you need to shower first?"

Shaking her head, she said, "Nope, I will use the guest bath; that way, you can go ahead and get ready for some night's rest." She smiled as she raised herself up on her tiptoes to kiss him lightly on the lips.

"I know your day has been hectic, and I am not about to ask anything like I was earlier. I got to go. I will see you in a few hours. Can you get the kids ready for school tomorrow just in case I run late?"

Caleb nodded and smiled as he walked toward the master ensuite. He looked down and thought *cold shower, my ass... with a fine woman walking out the door to go to work.* He wouldn't pester her. She had more than accommodated him.

Tonya called her team and asked what was up. They brought her up to date, informing her that they were still working on Project 2 and that the architectural drafts were still being debated with the graphic design department. Tonya made notes and took a few pages of design to review. She informed her night assistant not to disturb her under any circumstances. The night assistant nodded and walked away.

Tonya punched the code to her office and stared at two beautifully handcrafted cabinet doors, which hid a private elevator. Unbeknownst to the firm or the building code, Mike had created an elevator that was a direct link to their offices. The elevator only had three destinations: Mike's penthouse, her own office, and a private garage, which Mike only had access to, which led to a private entrance on a side street.

The cabinet doors opened, and Tonya's excitement was paramount in places where she had to prepare herself hours earlier for Caleb. Mike was short but muscularly built; she could look him in the eyes, but the life he lived coupled with their chemistry, to Tonya, he was the one she really wanted, and she was just bidding her time with Caleb.

3

THIRD PARTY

Mike looked at her. "It's 2 am Tonya, 2 am... do you know how that makes me feel? I am tired of being second to that loser of a husband you have..." Tonya said nothing as she walked up to him, dropped to her knees, unzipped his pants, and his complaints became moans. With each moan from Mike, Tonya savored the effect she had on him.

Mike's interest in Tonya's mind was like winning the lottery without purchasing the ticket. Many would say he was crazy... for wanting a woman with two kids. But being Mike, he was his own person. Not able to be a father biologically, he'd have the added bonus of children. The look of having it all...and Tonya, well, she gave him what he needed -business-wise as well in the bedroom. That had been hard to come by with his hidden taboos, which Tonya overlooked as part of the package life. He followed her train of thought. Tonya loved his lifestyle more than him, and it suited him.

Being brought up on the rough side of life, an ex-gangster turned millionaire- not all his adventures business-wise started clean. But to excel, which he did, he played the corporate world game and was looking to expand. He needed Tonya's mind... The woman had a knack for making pennies turn into millions. At least she had for him.

He looked down on her as she ministered to his needs. Yes, this is what he wanted, and he played to win. Always. Transitioning to the elevator, they traveled up to his penthouse and to his bedroom. Tonya received as much as she gave. This is where she really wanted to be...what she always wanted.

Mike, finally satiated, went to sleep. Tonya watched the rise and fall of his chest. Something she used to enjoy with Caleb, but things changed. Thinking about her upbringing... it was a life so different than what her single mother could provide for her and her three sisters. She hated the fact of sharing a room with all of her sisters and sleeping on a twin bed all of her life. Even though her kids will never have to experience her childhood, she observed Mike and noted that the average life with Caleb had become old. She rested her head upon Mike's chest, and his arms embraced her. Sleep blanketed over them for a few hours.

Rolling over to the nightstand to check the time on her phone, Tonya whispered in Mike's ear, "Baby, it's 6 am I got to go."

A disgruntled voice replied with the anticipation of this moment. "Why in the hell do you keep doing this to me?" Tonya released a guilty sigh as she flopped on her back, staring at the coffered ceiling.

"What do you even see in him? He can't provide for you and your children. He's a boring ass..."

"Mike, just stop!"

"Don't you tell me to stop. I am looking out for you, and quite frankly, I am tired of playing second fiddle."

"I told you that I am working on a plan to get out of that marriage."

"Well, let me help you out. I am opening a new office in South Carolina next month, and I want you to come with me. I will pay for your children to attend the best schools, and you will not have to want for anything."

"Next month!?! That is not enough time to..."

"To what?"

As the silence of the room became louder, Mike rolled over to grab a small box out of his nightstand. Tonya remained stiller than a corpse, thinking about how to buy more time. Mike began to sit up and pleaded with Tonya to do the same. Facing each other, Mike moved the small box from behind his back. Tonya's breathing became short and shallow as she heard the words marry me while staring at the 5.43 CT Vera Wang Platinum Princess Cut engagement ring.

"I'm not moving to South Carolina without you. You mean the world to me, and I want to give you everything that you deserve and more."

"I want that too, baby, but..." Tonya found it hard to find the words to speak what was really in her heart.

"Look, Tonya, I don't want to force you to do anything you don't want to do."

"But I do want this...us!" Tonya stated, looking at the ring and then Mike.

"Then show me. It's either him or me. I will no longer allow you to straddle the fence. You have three days to decide, or it's over between us."

Tonya leaned on the frame of the bedroom door. She watched Caleb sleeping so peacefully that she slightly began to regret her drastic actions to fulfill her mother's advice to never marry for love but for money. Tonya's mother's love for her father left her mother broke, busted, and disgusted. Tonya's mom vowed that she was not going to allow her daughters to repeat the same cycle. But Tonya, playing the role for ten years and after two children, she'd slightly grown to love Caleb. But it wasn't enough. She wanted it all... She wanted the life, the glam, and the security of living the life Mike had to offer. She walked toward the ensuite to shower since she hit the office gym after leaving Mike.

Tonya righted herself and walked forward. She stood a little longer inside the bedroom, pausing at the ensuite door as her thoughts took her back to their very first meeting.

Caleb stirred from his sleep to see his wife staring at him briefly before she turned toward the ensuite; her facial features told him so much as he masked his sleep.

His observation of her long hours and ongoing business

trips from work, along with all they had endured, made him feel Tonya's indifference. His mother's words hit him full force as he looked at his wife and felt the tables were turned. He had dismissed the thought for a while. Not wanting to believe what his intuition was beckoning him to see. The cold shower after the passionate lovemaking was the final straw. Dinner was where he had left it on the counter. *Why didn't she take it with her to work?*

The kids woke up around 5 am, an hour earlier than usual, stating they were hungry. Caleb asked questions and found out Tonya had rushed the children to bed with sandwiches. Yet the room was lit, and the atmosphere was on point. Her performance was stellar, and his libido was on a high as he thought of his good luck with work lately. The phone call that came soon after, as he headed for a cold shower, made him question *Is Tonya cheating on me?* The children's talk when they thought no one was listening drove the nail on the head.

He watched her close the door to their bathroom, and he felt the foreboding thought of loneliness. It hit him much like it did with his first love in Africa and having to leave his daughter behind. The signs were there. *God, not again,* Caleb thought as he looked up at the ceiling.

Endless thoughts ran through his mind as he called his wife's office soon after she arrived, only to receive a message from her assistant stating she was not to be disturbed. The call to her cell phone that went straight to voicemail fed a feeling of uncertainty-*What was so important that she couldn't answer her phone in the wee hours of the night to early morning...?*

His mind wandered to the past as Tonya wiped the sweat from her brow in the ensuite. Both of them thinking...

What now? Caleb remembered the female of his college days and Tonya looking at herself in the mirror, thought of Caleb, the well-to-do brother who changed her life...

4

❦

DATING AND GETTING TO KNOW

"Excuse me, do you have the time?" Tonya asked as she stopped Caleb in his tracks in the quad of AAMU. Not acknowledging who asked for the time, Caleb glanced down at his Rolex, and Tonya saw the dollar signs. She was a struggling college senior with no job prospects and was feeling the pressure from her mother to be a wife. Caleb was not only handsome, but he looked like money, and the closer she got to him, the more he smelled like money.

Unbeknownst to her, Caleb had spent two years working overseas after undergrad. He saved his non-taxable income earnings and was using the money to pay for grad school and to support the bundle of joy he had left there. His start-up business was thriving, and his master's degree would be completed at the end of the semester. All he desired now was a wife.

Caleb finally looked up, only to see a tall, slim, butter pecan complexion goddess.

Damn, he thought, as his mind hadn't mused over a woman since leaving Africa. Placing his emotions in check, Caleb subdued his thoughts about his past relationship. The female in front of him had caught his attention. Not completely throwing caution to the wind, his physical mind reminded him that it had been a while since he entertained a woman... in the biblical sense.

Thinking about her question, he rechecked his watch to regain his composure....

"It's a quarter to six," he replied.

"Thank you. I left my watch and cell phone in the dorm, and I felt totally lost."

Dorm room, Caleb thought. Tonya looked too mature to be living in a dorm room. He could have sworn that she was a grad student, too. Seizing the moment, he pried to unlock her age mystery.

"I understand. Can you imagine going back to the times before we had cell phones," he said with a smile. "Or are you too young and always had a cell phone?"

Tonya was a smitten kitten as she let out a light laugh.

"I remember the days of buying minutes for cell phones and unlimited talk and text after nine pm and on the weekends."

"Okay, okay. You know a little."

"Just a little," she replied.

"Uhm...," Caleb debated within himself. What could he say

next? Caleb realized there was a slim chance of him running into this beautiful woman again, who was causing electricity to flow through his body. It was now or never, and he decided that it was now.

"Forgive me if I am being too forward, but you are a beautiful woman, and I would love to take you to dinner."

Tonya was used to getting attention from men, but this attention was different. It seemed pure yet purposeful. Not the attention that usually landed her regretting the actions of the night.

"You don't even know my name." Caleb reached for Tonya's hand.

"I assumed it was Angel because standing in your presence feels like heaven."

Bracing her fall from his mesmerizing touch, Tonya held it together. She had never been referred to as an angel. The pickup lines she was used to hearing referred to her hourglass figure.

"That's cute, cheesy but cute."

Caleb and Tonya laughed at his humor with his pickup line.

"Cheesy, but I mean it. I'm enjoying this moment."

"My name is Tonya." she smiled.

"Nice to meet you, Tonya. I am Caleb."

"Nice to meet you, too."

Tonya accepted the dinner invitation, and the two later dined at the Rocket City's most popular steakhouse. This was a step up from the campus cafe where all her college dates had been held.

Caleb was the perfect gentleman, and dinner included

their personal stories of family struggles, future aspirations, and desire for marriage. While finishing up the last semester of their individual degrees, they became inseparable. Tonya had practically moved in with Caleb after a month of daily dinner and study dates at Caleb's two-bedroom condo just outside the city. The two discussed future plans of excelling individually and as a power couple after graduation.

After three months of dating, Caleb became mesmerized by the relationship and all that it was promising. Tonya's values of marriage and family were strongly suggestive and fed his inner desire. She asked him for nothing as women had done in the past. *When you know, you know,* Caleb thought, and he proposed, and Tonya accepted. Not wanting to wait, the two eloped to Vegas. Life was grand.

His wife was so excited about the life he had created. Caleb loved Tonya's enthusiasm and support as he worked to make life for them better. She was a go-getter. Her own ambition matched his, and they were a force with which to be reckoned. He had the house, the money, and the woman. Tonya had gained a provider. Tonya couldn't believe how lucky she had gotten, for he was all she wanted.

His dreams of wanting the good life only fueled her to press for more. She was enthralled, but she truly loved the life he was offering. Children were not an issue as they were, in her eyes, an investment should things go south, as she had learned from her family members still living on government assistance.

However, she strived for her life to be different. Tonya wanted more, not only from her husband but for herself. Seeing all that Caleb had to offer, including his loyalty to family, not only had she gained a provider for herself... but she also gained a daughter, a son, and a master's degree that came in the years to follow. Tonya enjoyed what only women dreamed about; the experience of a traditional marriage where the man took care of all the household bills and all the aspects of family life and leisure, leaving the wife's income to do as she pleased.

As fate would have it, the vows, *for better or for worse,* came with the changes in the economy, causing Caleb's business to belly up. Caleb, being practical, took a job in sales immediately to keep funds flowing; however, he could no longer maintain their lifestyle with his income alone. He continued to look for better employment and changes in the economy to earn more. However, Caleb had to witness his wife take on what he considered his responsibility, and it hurt him to the core.

Tonya, at first, bided her time, waiting for Caleb to get back on his feet. But as time went on, she began to silently resent him. Caleb felt the disdain in her sidebar looks, which made him feel like less than a man at times. He was doing all that he could, but he saw Tonya's respect for him dwindle.

On some days, Caleb questioned if she genuinely saw him. In those moments, he wondered if she ever really loved him or just the life he offered when they met. The internal conflict that they each felt broke down the quality areas of their relationship. Each of them wanted more out of the life they were living... but the difference in areas was like the parting of the Red Sea in their relationship. They each were on different shores looking from across the sea as the water began to fall back from the force that was keeping the inevitable at bay.

Caleb wanted her again, the woman he first met -the wife when he said *I do*. While Tonya pictured Caleb as he would never be in her eyes.

The belief of a young girl in college had become a woman who wanted more than what her husband had to offer. She had evolved to see the opportunities that were available as she became a working woman. Being the involuntary breadwinner, Tonya found a breadwinner in Mike when she landed a job at his company after Caleb lost his business.

Caleb recognized it was just a matter of time. He had hoped that the last few months of productive progress would get him back on his feet to make up for the lost time and revenue that was once so lucrative and save his marriage. But as Caleb watched, his wife closed the bathroom door. He felt his time had run out.

Tonya walked out of the ensuite to see Caleb looking dead at her. She saw hurt in his eyes. But being undaunted... she was ready to leave her old money for new money and accept Mike's proposal.

Several days passed by, and Tonya was still trying to work up her nerve to talk to Caleb. Her confidence waned, and her voice dried in her throat when Caleb looked at her the night she came home with Mike's diamond in her locked briefcase.

Walking into the house after work, expecting to see Caleb with the children, Tonya came home to find the children sitting at the dinner table with her father-in-law. Mr. Mitchell looked at her and kept his thoughts to himself. He thought of his wife lying in a hospital bed and her son. He was aware that God would have the last say. But he couldn't hold his peace. Being respectful to the children and not saying anything, he turned his back to the children and looked at Tonya curiously.

Tonya wasn't ashamed of her actions, and she knew very little about God. Growing up, her mother didn't place much emphasis on church or religion as she did survival through means of money.

But Caleb's father she feared. She was not scared, but she feared him as if he was like God. He was what she didn't see in Caleb. She recognized his authority and power was above money. A man like Mr. Mitchell she couldn't handle. It was as if he saw what she was thinking when she wanted no one else to know.

The children watched her as they had had enough of Grandpa themselves. They waited quietly to be excused. Mr. Mitchell loved his grandchildren but tolerated no disrespect, and video games were far from his mind.

His eyes dismissed the spiritual revelation of his soon-to-be ex-daughter-in-law as he turned around and told the children to go clean their rooms. They groaned, looking for Tonya to save them. She said nothing as her tongue was caught and her lips were sealed.

Mr. Mitchell made a sound to silence them and pulled their gaming consoles to the middle of the table. "After your rooms are clean and after I have said my goodbyes, these will be on the table. Give your mom a hug and proceed to do as I mentioned."

Each child gave Tonya a hug and walked to their room, leaving the adults to talk. Mr. Mitchell voiced loudly. "Close your doors," as he wished to talk to Tonya in private. Tonya walked to the fridge and took out one bottle of water, declining the hospitality of asking for her father-in-law's preference.

Mr. Mitchell disregarded her blatant disrespect unmoved. He silently prayed, and God brought to his remembrance Ephesian 6:12.

For we wrestle not against flesh and blood, but against princi-palities, against powers, against the rulers of the darkness of this world, against spiritual wickedness in high places.

He watched Tonya, the epitome of what brings a good man to waste. *A woman who brings grief due to fleshly desires and inevitably brings shame upon herself, her husband, and her children. Whoredom has no place with God, as she has done,* he thought. But as it stood. She is his son's mate. A woman he and his wife would not have approved of, and Caleb never gave them the opportunity to meet her before marrying.

His beloved wife, as spiteful as she can be, was at least an honest woman, a faithful woman, who was *his and his* alone in all their years of marriage. Mr. Mitchell thought about his wife's past experiences. He had to be a real man before her, a safe haven, a place of peace so she could be herself, and he could not forsake her. He had to love her as Christ loved the church. In him, she could safely trust in the areas that gave her trauma and pain. And she loved him in her own way. For even in her pain, she gave him a son, Caleb.

Mr. Mitchell didn't take for granted the measure of sacrifice placed upon her well-being when she discovered she carrying his son. But to him and to him alone, she showed him how deep her love was to give him a child. He knew she would be incapable of more, but Caleb was a gift. A gift his wife sacrificed for him. It emotionally tore at her - the only pregnancy her body could handle was a male child. A daughter she could have loved without shame. She would have had the opportunity to become a champion of what she lost as a female growing up. But she took it in stride. Mr. Mitchell saw the toll and what the lack of love did to Caleb and his wife. Mr. Mitchell, thankful for God's blessings, realized he had to stay in constant prayer over the situation.

Refocusing his mind, Mr. Mitchell observed his son's wife. He saw her brokenness, watched the inner aspect of her spirit... and pondered over what she didn't see in herself. He discerned that her inner desires would be fulfilled, and she would embrace it; even if it would be hell wide open to live it, she'd live it without remorse. She was a piece of work, a demon-possessed woman driven by an evil ambition, motivated by greed, lust, and deceit, full of pride and self-love to the detriment of her family, her children, and her eternal soul damned without change. Mr. Mitchell swiped off imaginary lint from his trousers, not looking at her as he spoke his mind.

"So, you are going to divorce my son now, right?"

Tonya almost choked on her water as she had not mentioned her thoughts to Caleb. Tonya thought.... *Is Caleb thinking of divorce?* As if Mr. Mitchell read her thoughts.

He continued. "Caleb doesn't involve me with your marital affairs. I just see the spirit of adulteress all over you."

Tonya couldn't stand her in-laws. They were like psychic or something. Caleb was enough, but he was like a baby compared to his parents. Not to be put off, she tilted her head and raised her bottle to him before answering.

"And If I was too?"

He again overlooked her haughtiness. "How often will I be able to see my grandchildren? How soon are you leaving for another state, South Carolina, or," he paused, "North Carolina? Ah yes," as he watched her, "South."

Tonya looked at him, confused. *How does he know me like this? See this right here,* Tonya thought, *This is the final nail to leave Caleb. This Mombo jumbo psychic stuff!*

Tonya wanted no more parts of it. Mike was an atheist, and she was happy about it, especially after dealing with 'The Mitchells'. Tonya, wanting to end the conversation, completed his thoughts.

"Yes, I'm sure you will when they visit Caleb."

"How about when they don't?"

"Yes, Mr. Mitchell, I will make sure they know and spend time with you until they are grown and are off to college. Okay... you satisfied now?"

Mr. Mitchell looked at her as if to say I hold you to that or else. Tonya swallowed a sip of water and looked out the window from across the room. Dumbfounded over the whole conversation that just took place, she was waiting for the opportunity to leave the room. Hearing the back door open was like an old Rolaids commercial. How do you spell relief...

Caleb walked in, happy to see his father still at the

table. "Sorry Dad, it took longer than expected, but I'm happy to see you still here. Hi Tonya."

She waved and left the room smiling at Caleb, which wasn't for him but for her sheer joy to be excused. Mr. Mitchell watched her leave, then turned to his son.

"How you doing Caleb? I'm concerned about you son."

"I'm good as good can be Dad, and that's all I'm going to say." Mr. Mitchell nodded.

"No need to say more, but son, remember this...Proverbs 10:8. "

His father pointed to where Tonya exited, held up his hands as to say not my place to say more, and walked toward the garage door. Caleb laughed and wondered what manner of cursing had occurred Biblically toward Tonya with his father's quoted scripture. It made him wonder what had taken place before he entered. Caleb watched his father leave only to re-enter the house and call out to the children, "Grandpa loves you. I'm leaving now."

Bedroom doors opened, and the children rushed out to give their Granddad a hug. Wanting to please him, they talked about how clean their rooms were and pulled on him to inspect them before he left.

Caleb smiled as the children waved goodbye to Mr. Mitchell, and he praised them for having clean rooms. Waving goodbye, he walked out and closed the garage door.

Caleb, seeing his father gone, took out his phone and read the Bible scripture. Knowing his father, it was a foreboding sign of a discussion that was being held at bay. It continued to get worse for Caleb.

He feared what most men felt when faithful... Why was he

facing the situation of losing his wife and children, in addition to the life built- the house, the car, and ultimately, his faith in the intuition of marriage. Not to mention his pride as a man so commonplace these days.

5

PENDING DIVORCE OR PUT ASUNDER

At six pm, Caleb came home thinking about his latest sales project with Sanchez Inc., which wasn't going as well as he'd liked, to seeing his children crying as Tonya was packing up their belongings and putting them in boxes. The children ran to him in tears as he walked into the house.

"Dad, Mom is packing up our stuff, saying we are leaving and you are not coming and that we are going to live with her boss, Uncle Mike." Caleb stood listening, hearing what wasn't spoken to him. Most of what his children said hit him so hard that he found it hard to breathe. Uncle Mike? He thought. *So that's his name, and she's had my children around some other man. My daughter included?* Caleb wanted to confront Tonya that instant. But he held it in check for the sake of his children.

He did what he could only do. Gathered his children to

him and reassured them that all would be okay. He ushered them into the living room and noticed the PS 5 was still connected. "Here, you two play on the gaming system. Have you eaten yet?" They shook their heads no. Caleb kissed their foreheads. Dinner will be... he paused, hearing the tape dispenser. "Just sit here, ok. Don't bother your mom; she's busy. I'm going to make arrangements for dinner." They looked at him and nodded.

His son, then asked. "Are you okay with us leaving?"

Caleb held back his emotions, which became harder to do as time ticked by, and he heard the clear tape pull and cut from the other side of the house. It was like gunshots heard on a deathly still night.

"No, son. I'm not ok. But I have to get you dinner, right?"

His son nodded and was happy to hear his father's thoughts. Caleb avoided the children's room with Tonya. It was taking all he had not to confront her. Knowing how he felt it would not be in the best interest of the children. He entered the bedroom shared with Tonya. He thought of the last time they had sex, and it hit him harder than he thought. He silenced and stopped the train of thought. He needed a distraction, and the children needed to eat, but they ultimately had to leave the house. He didn't trust himself to remain calm with Tonya.

He called his father. "Dad, how is mom?"

His father stated she was fine and was just transported to a senior living facility for a few weeks of therapy before she would be allowed to come home. Caleb was thankful to hear that as he asked his father to come and pick up the children.

He finally broke down and told his father about his speculations of a pending divorce and what he had come home to.

"I'm sorry to hear this, son. I was heading your way. Something told me to be in your area. I'll be there in 10 minutes. I'm just around the corner. Have the children had dinner?"

"No."

"Okay, I'll take them out; let them know I'm coming. Also, Caleb?"

"Yeah, Dad."

"Let me keep them for a few days; you two will need that. Are you and Tonya going to be okay?"

"I can't answer that one, Dad, but I have no intentions of laying my hands on her maliciously if that's what you're asking. I've been waiting for the bottom to drop. Just not like this."

Tonya entered the room as he got off the phone. She started to talk, but the look Caleb gave her made her step back and be quiet. Tonya had never seen that look on Caleb. But she knew of it from the men her mother had dealt with. There is a part of a man a woman should never poke, and Caleb was radiating that part like a nuclear bomb waiting to go off. They stared at each other, and she dropped her eyes.

"My father is taking the children for two days- pack their things."

Tonya, not liking his tone, was about to protest, and Caleb stood up from his sitting position and was in her face in seconds. In a deathly quiet, still voice, just above a whisper, Caleb spoke his mind... "Woman, I have never laid a finger on you. Don't push me further than your insolence has already pushed."

Tonya looked up at him as if to say try it. Her look pushed a button, and Caleb wrapped his hands around her throat and squeezed, then dropped them when he heard the children in the other room. Tonya coughed to breathe and walked out of the room. Feeling her legs somewhat faint. She stumbled as she reached out with her hand and touched the wall to steady herself. She was livid as she turned the corner and did as she was told.

She walked into the children's rooms, preparing their things, and heard her father-in-law enter the house. She began to have second thoughts of leaving. What was she about to get herself into by leaving. Caleb, the man-child she saw with her eyes, had become a man in an instant with his stance, and it frightened her. She didn't expect Caleb to remove the children from the home to have their conversation.

She was scared to be alone with him. His look of loathing and disgust was evident as he stared at her in their bedroom. She deserved it. But she didn't want it. She wanted to think of herself as the victim for marrying him and him not providing her the life she wanted. She wanted to place him in the same category as all the lovers her mother had socially entertained. But Caleb was none of those men. He was just not financially stable, and he allowed her to be. *But I want more than this, family life, more than what we had before financially.* She thought as she walked out to see the children off.

The children gave her a hug as they said their goodbyes to go with their Granddad. They were concerned about their parents. The daughter, not wanting to give too much away to her younger brother, understood things were not looking good. Still, she kept it to herself and looked at her father for reassurance. Caleb kissed and hugged them and put on a great show; all was okay. The children looked at their mom; they saw Tonya's fear. The daughter knew her Mom had some explaining to do. The youngest saw the fear as when they had to tell the truth and the fear of having to speak it. The youngest ran back to her.

"Love you mom. Do the right thing, ok? Like you tell us. Dad says it's all going to be okay, and he doesn't want us to leave him." Tonya nodded. She did not say a word as her father-in-law looked at her like I wish you would say something. Then, he ushered the children out the door. He turned to them both.

"I want your children to see you just like they left you. Remember that," and he turned and took his leave. Praying for the best and expecting the worst as divorce always leaves mental alternatives for the children. The house became quiet as both adults waited until the car left the driveway.

Caleb turned to the bedroom and took a shower to cool off. Tonya knew touching a box, and any sound thereof would not be in her best interest. She sat in the living room in the dark, hearing the shower run. Eventually, she selected wine from the hidden cabinet cooler, picked out a stemmed glass, and then opened a bottle of wine. As she sipped and swallowed the last from her first glass, she jumped upon hearing the sound of his voice.

"Pour me a glass."

Caleb stood before her, a 6 ft 2 in height man in a t-shirt and sweats. Muscularly built, the t-shirt hugged his torso, showing his mid-pack tone, and the sweat pants, although baggy, rested on areas showing enough of an impression for the lustful eye. Even with a pending divorce, Tonya found him quite attractive. He was a handsome man.

Her lust was getting the best of her with alcohol in her system. Divorce or no divorce, sex wasn't an issue with her, mad, happy, or sad. Retrieving him a glass, she filled it halfway and handed it to him. Caleb took the glass and drowned it.

"Pour me another."

Tonya watched him. She did not like the idea of him with alcohol in his system and the inner beast clearly sitting in the wings of his demeanor, but she didn't protest. She poured. They continued drinking until the bottle was empty.

Neither were feeling the full effects of the alcohol. But both were in their thoughts. Tonya, suffering from mental instability, sipped her wine in denial. The alcohol-fueled her incapacity to see the truth about the situation. She was lustful, almost to an addiction, as she looked at Caleb. She understood physically when it came to a man. Her mother had taught her well. Physically, she found him attractive, but unlike her mother, she would let him go for the sake of her own endeavors. Money was her god.

Caleb was seething mad. If he could, he would beat some sense into Tonya, but he couldn't beat the mess out of her. Not being able to see her as he wanted to remember her in the younger years of marriage, he envisioned Tonya as someone less than the mother of his children, unworthy to be his wife. She was changing into something else in his mind, which was becoming more apparent, and it didn't sit well with him. He thought of another man having what was rightfully, lawfully, and in the sight of God his. He hated the thoughts running through his mind that made the woman before him turn sordid and ugly, vile and disgusting. He looked at her loathing, and his mind snapped. Thinking back on all he had endured for the sake of the family. He looked at her... as she became a slut, a whore. In biblical terms, her very presence screamed Jezebel, a gold digger in his view. The words in his mind came forth in his facial expressions, and they brought Tonya back to reality.

Although he didn't speak the words, Tonya saw his demeanor, and she felt the power. He was seething mad, and she liked it. She resented her years of being the breadwinner. She wanted him to suffer. But Caleb kept his composure as he brought his thoughts under control, and Tonya watched, interestingly waiting. Watching for signs that fed into her wishes for him.

"So, Mike, is it?" She nodded and quietly answered his onslaught of questions while enjoying a glimpse into his pain.

"Are there any more than him?"

"No."

He chuckled as if to say yeah, right. Only to ask... "I assume you've slept with him?"

"Yes." Caleb looked at her; hurt clearly slipped into his demeanor, along with more anger.

She smirked as she looked at him.

"Have you slept with others besides him recently?"

Wanting to dig into his clearly seen wound, she answered quickly and with a strong voice and tone...*You,* she said sarcastically to get a reaction out of him. Caleb smiled as he noticed her cat-and-mouse game with his emotions. Shaking his head at her antics, Caleb pulled from his sweatpants a folded piece of paper. A paper he kept to himself for the past year. Forgiving his wife, knowing she had done so much for the family. But in light of the present situation, it burned in his hands. Seeing his controlled stance, Tonya became a little fearful. Caleb was looking at the paper as he asked his next question.

"How often did the children see him?"

He glanced at her, waiting, with the paper in one hand and the glass in the other. Tonya looked at the paper and saw the logo. She shook her head, not wanting to answer. Caleb threw his glass across the room, and she heard the shattering of glass. Her body jerked from the reaction and the intensity of his tone.

"Answer me, dammit. I deserve to know."

Tonya looked at him; not wanting to appear weak, she defiantly stated, once a month. Caleb looked at her as if to say continue. Tonya looked at the paper and continued to talk.

"Caleb, when I took them to work. You know," she paused, "Mike, my boss." She stopped herself from saying more as she gauged Caleb's mood.

It registered with Caleb. The late-night work, the nightly texts, and interrupted family time due to the boss calling. *It was him!* "How often did you sleep with him, Tonya? More than once, I assume." Holding up the piece of paper. Tonya looked at the medical report, a paper she wondered where she had left it, only to see that Caleb had it all this time. She nodded. Caleb wanted to know the numerous rendezvous of her relationship as it alluded to the paper, but didn't want to know at the same time. Considering it was a past situation, he discovered it and had already confronted Tonya. So, he changed the next question, as the children gave insight into a time period. Caleb thought back to when Tonya truly began to change, and it became more evident as he asked the questions.

"For how long Tonya? How long have you been sleeping with him?" Caleb asked, not wanting it all to be true.

"Two years," she said simply.

Caleb closed his eyes, hearing the timeframe. He held up the medical report. "So was this one mine, or you don't know, considering your activities."

"Yours."

Caleb dropped the paper to the floor. Tonya looked at the header Plan Parenthood Clinic. Caleb had to ask again in light of her recent activities... "So, the one 5 years ago?"

"Not yours Caleb."

Caleb felt the wave of grief as if it were new when he learned about the abortion of the twins Tonya aborted 5 years ago. He forgave her after finding out the twins were not his. It took a lot out of him, knowing she had cheated on a girl's trip with her sisters. He knew of her background and how her sisters were. But this, a second abortion again without his knowledge and blatant infidelity, and this time without any remorse from her, as her sisters admitted to setting her up.

Caleb was struggling to accept, and forgiveness was becoming difficult to obtain with all that was occurring and being stated. Caleb stared at a wall, collecting his thoughts. He spoke barely above a whisper.

"This," holding up the medical report, "happened a year ago. But you have been with this man and myself for more than 2 years." Caleb's voice escalated upward and deep. Caleb looked at her with questions still lingering…. thinking of the present day.

"So, that night, you left to go work just a few days ago, Tonya-You slept with him after sleeping with me?"

Tonya was waiting for this question to hurt him more. "Yes!" She stated and gave a description of the night. Caleb looked at her, and every name and emotion that washed over him that made his wife vile screamed in his mind. Tonya's words and actions shattered his sacred image of her as the mother of his children. His inner thoughts of her and the silent inward prayer to overlook her faults to make the marriage work, yet again after knowing what she had done.

Caleb's emotions surfaced; thinking about life and the acknowledgment of its existence was a remnant piece of paper held in his hands. "Then *HOW THE HELL DO YOU KNOW IF THE ABORTION* was mine or his… a year ago?" Caleb asked vehemently.

Tonya was gleeful on the inside as she saw what she had been waiting for… a deep hurt and wretched pain etched in his eyes. Tonya smiled widely as she made her following statement.

"He can't have children."

Caleb looked at her with a newfound hatred. He had prayed she would change her mind. But as she started giving an account of what she had done in detail, he knew Tonya, his wife, was gone. This Tonya became more transparent, and she changed right before his eyes. The silence was loud in the room as she made her last statement, leaving them to their thoughts as to what was...

"Do you love him?"

Caleb asked, breaking the silence. Tonya heard the question and laughed. She pondered over it. Inwardly, she asked that question, and being honest with herself, she took a sip of wine, looked at Caleb, and made her final point.

"What's love got to do with it?"

Caleb stared at her, and his inner beast within could not be contained. "We have children, Tonya! Did you ever think of them!" He bellowed.

"I am Caleb. We deserve better than this. I'm tired of taking up the slack for you!"

"Slack! It takes two to make this marriage work. Beyond finances Tonya."

Caleb looked dumbfounded, only to then speak about the elephant in the room.

"Oh, so you married me for my money? That's it, huh... typical gold digger... I fell for an open, honest, no-shame gold digger that was just packaged nicely to fit my needs as long as I delivered!"

Tonya played the role. As long as he would deliver the life she wanted, she wasn't ashamed to admit it. Caleb finally understood. Why the children were neglected by her. They were her meal ticket if things went south. But the tables had turned. She was the primary breadwinner, and she resented it. The years of inadequacy that he felt hit him hard as he stood thinking. He allowed himself to embrace the truth of her lack of support when things took a turn for the worse.

The silent you ain't a man attitude she gave - it came at him in full force. She was a demon!

There wasn't an action within his power to revive his loss except the lottery. And if he made the money, Tonya would be an empty living soul in regards to a married life with him. What he thought he had was a lie from the beginning. He looked at Tonya, thinking of how he could hurt her as she stabbed the knife into his heart. But Caleb admitted to himself he couldn't harm her, at least not physically.

Out of spite, he walked up to her as she put her glass down to leave the room. He grabbed her by the waist and pulled her to him. She was nothing more than an instrument of destruction. Tonya felt powerful as she looked at him face to face. Delusional, her lust got the best of her... She smelled his scent and the hint of wine mixed with the heightened adrenaline on his breath. A scent that aroused her, kicking her libido to an all-time high. She heard his words and smiled inwardly as she saw it hurt him.

"So, you don't love him like you don't love me."

She looked at his face, searching for his hurt; to add insult to injury, she smiled and leaned forward into his embrace and lightly touched his lips. Caleb released her, placing his hands on her shoulders to ask the next question.

"So, this body of *YOURS* is open to be used as he and I both saw fit. That's it! *RIGHT* Tonya?"

As his hands reached up around her throat. Holding her in place. Tonya placed her hands upon his, not liking the way things were going.

"Let me go, Caleb," Tonya whispered.

Caleb held her firmly, controlling Tonya with his hands

around her neck; he leaned in and kissed her roughly. She took it and returned it- as it was as she wanted...

Tonya deepened the kiss, and his hands slipped around her waist, lifting her. Caleb held Tonya's 5-foot-7 slender frame and moved them across the room until she felt the cold wall to the entrance of their bedroom against her back. His hands became free to roam, and he aligned his body, pressing against hers, holding her in place.

His hands found what he wanted as he lifted one of her legs to his waist, holding her against him and the wall. He kissed her as his hand freed himself and explored her and felt her wet and ready. As God commanded a man and his wife to become one, Caleb's pent-up anger was vented.

Tonya wrapped her legs around him, her arms laced around his neck. Caleb braced himself and manhandled her as he repeatedly became one with her forcefully. As if waiting and on cue, with the first moan of arousal escaping Tonya's lips, Caleb disengaged as he released the seed of his labor and whispered in her ear.

"The mother of my children is a prostitute."

Tonya went rigid as her mind became clear and registered his statement. He released his hold as she stood there aroused and unsatisfied. Caleb looked her up and down... as he stepped back, looking at her like she was a piece of meat.

Still showing, his arousal was waning as he looked at her with disgust. He saw the tears fall from her face. His look made her feel used and worthless at that moment. She watched as he took a corner of her shirt to clean himself. The gesture registered in her mind that his love for her had waxed cold.

She watched the look of admiration and appreciation, even in her worst moment with him, die behind his eyes. That look Tonya knew all too well. She had seen it first at the tender age of ten, only to understand it better at age fifteen.

Tonya remembered the look on the older men's faces as they started the night with her mother using her mother's body only to then drug her to sleep and finish off the night with her older sister minutes later.

The look Caleb gave was a look she never wanted to be directed toward herself. Yet here Caleb stood. Lustful and vicious. She wanted him to stay a man-child in her eyes. Not this male before her. Not this unforgiving user. This man she couldn't control. Tonya knew, at that moment, she couldn't play the victim. Her mother was wrong, and Tonya saw for a fleeting moment a glitch in her well-designed ideology of life.

Caleb, seeing what he wanted in her facial expression, turned his back to her, walked into their bedroom, and closed the door. Tonya heard it click as he locked her out, which unleashed a pain she didn't realize existed, but it would only last for a moment.

Tonya slid to the floor and cried. She thought of Mike and then every man that came to her house during her childhood. Then she spoke her mind... "F.U Caleb!" She screamed.

"F.U. *I'M GOING TO LIVE MY BEST LIFE WITHOUT YOU!*"

F.U., she said over and over again, calling him everything but a child of God. She waited, wanting a reaction, as she wallowed in her own pain, but all she heard was silence. Caleb listened to her cry, and he waited. Like his mother, Tonya, the crying woman would stop. And on cue, the crying stopped, and then she screamed and called him out of his name. He sat on the bed, listening, knowing Tonya wanted a reaction. She eventually pounded her fist on the door, demanding that he open it. But that, too, came to an end.

He had lived this all his life. He had his mother to thank. Tonya was just another chain squeezing out his inner peace, locking him away from love. He looked toward the ceiling. *GOD, I NEED YOU!* He silently prayed for forgiveness and stayed locked in the room.

It was 4 am when he emerged. Tonya was asleep on the sofa with a bottle of vodka on the table, ¾ empty. He walked over to her. She had taken a shower and was dressed in shorts and a t-shirt. She was a beautiful woman aesthetically. Her body was fine even with past pregnancies. He looked around the room, dismissing her. She had swept away the glass debris and cleaned the kitchen. Feeling the chill of the room, he went to the linen closet, pulled out a blanket, and covered her.

She was still the mother of his children. He reminded himself, and the chains around his heart squeezed a little more, and then his third firewall was built around his thoughts of love... He thought of his mother, Liana's mother, Katura, who was in Africa and now his soon-to-be ex-wife. *God why?* He asked as he returned to the bedroom and locked the door. Troubled sleep finally came.

6

BROKEN

Tonya sat on a sofa in Mike's office, looking apprehensive. "He might not let me leave the state." Mike ignored Tonya's insight into the situation as he happily looked at the ring on her finger. She was finally going to be all his. Mike looked at her, thinking of what he wanted to do to her if work wasn't pressing for his time. His thoughts and reality reached a point, and he actually heard her calling his name...unfortunately, it wasn't as he imagined.

Shifting in his seat, he looked at her... "Look, Tonya, as long as I know you leaving him for me, I can wait. He agreed to the divorce, right?"

Tonya nodded. She still had things to work through, but not wanting to lose Mike in the process, she wore the ring at work, but only in Mike's presence. Caleb had become cold and indifferent except in front of the children. He was waiting for her. Caleb made it clear it was her issue and her burden to finish what she started. She slept on the sofa at night as their bedroom door locks had changed, and all her belongings were in boxes in the living room. She had yet to say the words divorce to Caleb.

Mike, knowing how Tonya handled business closures, handed her a business card.

Accepting the card, Tonya questioned, *what does Mike want now?*

Mike walked away as she read the bold words: Divorce Attorney at Law. She swallowed the lump in her throat.

"Michael...?" She whined a little, calling him by his given name to plead her case.

He cut her off. "Tomorrow at 10am, their office is expecting you; your appointment is with a dear friend of mine, Kalbowski."

Tonya nodded. She had no room for debate when it came to Mike, unlike Caleb, which had surprisingly changed in the last few days. Caleb was not the Caleb she thought she knew.

Mike looked at her sternly, "I need to see the papers in progress for the petition. Next week, I'm off to South Carolina. I need to know the business with you is personally in progress. I want severance. When are you moving out, or will he?"

Tonya stalled. "We are working to tell the children. It's not that simple, Mike."

Mike paused in reviewing a purchase order. "What do you mean... Are you still sleeping with him and playing house, Tonya?"

"No, Mike. The kids have been told I'm moving with you

and that they are coming too. But he's their father, and he has rights. They love him."

Mike kept his inner judgments to himself. *The Children*, he thought. *They are going to be mine, not that loser's blood or no blood*. Mike thought. *I am going to make it so.* Mike stated inwardly, saying nothing to Tonya as his secretary, Mr. Thomas, beeped in on the intercom system, announcing Ms. Mitchell's 3 o'clock appointment was in the conference room. Mike walked her to the door and kissed her lightly. Tonya left, and Mike stood looking at the closed door in thought. Then, he called Mr. Samuel, chairman of the board for Sanchez Inc., and enjoyed a pleasant conversation in lieu of some business liaisons. The call ended with Mr. Samuel assuring Mike he would make some inquiries and to be expecting a call. Later in the day, Mike received a return call from a high-ranking sales department manager, Mr. Bradley.

"Hi, Mr. Emerson, Mr. Bradley here. My supervisor informed me of your interest in a bill of sales for your up-and-coming opening in the Hilton Head area of South Carolina?"

Mike smiled. "Yes.... I wanted to speak with you about your latest project. I noticed a few things and want some insight. We are about to embark upon a few projects with my new business location in South Carolina. I know I could use your advice."

Mr. Bradley, Caleb's direct supervisor, gave his opinion. Mike listened to the information and stated. "Mr. Bradley, I love your thoughts. I don't want to work with anyone but you on this project and the new project you have with Sanchez Inc. I hear you are having a few issues. Let me make a suggestion. I will send you a business client I know who can handle that personally."

Mr. Bradley knew a project with Mike Emerson would be a massive boost for his quarterly sales, not to mention the yearly bonus if he worked on it personally. Mr. Bradley looked at the spreadsheet before him, and the slight boost that he was excited about with Mr. Mitchell was minuscule in comparison to what Mr. Emerson was offering.

He heard himself say without hesitation. "Mr. Emerson, I look forward to working closely with you on this and meeting with your business personnel who can help with the issues we have at hand. Mr. Samuel and myself will be in touch. Thank you."

Mike ended the call, beaming brightly, knowing the damage he had done. Tonya and Caleb would be no more. Knowing Tonya, this would be the last straw. Mike left for South Carolina, knowing Caleb's life would take a turn for the worse in a few weeks. He gave Tonya's divorce lawyer a key to one of his real estate properties, a 3200 square foot interior-designed, furnished home in her children's school district. He wanted her away from Caleb. She had no excuses to still be with him. And when the hammer dropped for Caleb, unbeknownst to Tonya, she would have an outlet without Caleb's input.

⸻

Three weeks passed, and Tonya and Caleb made the best of the situation. Filing for separation as they worked to separate financial assets. Caleb, although financially strapped for immediate cash on hand and living expenses, had an impressive financial portfolio. Tonya wanted her piece of the pie and did not want to leave the marriage without some assets of her own. Caleb's parents held most of his inheritance in a trust. So, Caleb's finances, except those created during the marriage, were not available to Tonya, and the children would not have access until age 25. Tonya was livid, but she had no other recourse options.

Due to his income over the years, if Caleb had full custody, Tonya would be held liable for child support. Her lawyer stated if her spouse was without a stable income or a job, she could also be liable for alimony due to the nature of the divorce and her infidelity in question.

Tonya knew filing for separation would be best. Mike hated it. But he was not above the law. Mike scolded himself for messing with Caleb's employment. But he also felt it was worth it for Tonya to move forward with his plans.

Caleb got a call from his supplier stating the Sanchez project was to be handled by a different agent. Also, he was served with a notice that after he finalized all active contracts, their business and services with him would no longer be needed. His work, while impeccable, the company stated they were going in a different direction.

Mr. Bradley and a few other executive officials hated to see him go, but the millions of contracts that came with Emerson could not be passed up.

Caleb looked at the 1-year severance pay and the impressive letter of reference. If only he had gotten this 9 months ago. While searching for another job, he and Tonya would probably still be together. Reflecting on the whole ordeal,

God, you are interesting. Caleb smiled slightly as his spiritual eye gained awareness of GOD WILL PROVIDE. Sometimes, God will remove that which is not suitable for you and make way for something expected but previously denied. He was wondering how he was going to make ends meet with Tonya, threatening to move out. Caleb knew he didn't have a job and wouldn't be able to keep the house.

Caleb, after receiving the severance package, immediately filed for unemployment and placed his earnings, after taxes, into an investment account, which he used for living expenses and paid for a 6 months lease on an apartment. He gave a portion to Tonya for the children by a signed document filed with their attorneys.

They finally filed for divorce and agreed with much animosity that the children would be with Tonya while pending custody orders from the court. Tonya could not leave the state, which kept them separated, and the divorce pending as custodial rights and Mike's meddling took its toll for the worst lasted beyond a year, leaving Caleb broken spiritually and emotionally. Caleb became a changed man.

Caleb visited his mother in an upscale senior care facility. Hating to see her in pain, as she had suffered another stroke and was in recovery again. Her mind was still sharp, although her body was taking its toll. She looked at him.

"Well, what you looking crazy for? You knew that woman was no good when you met her, or at least you should have."

"Not today, Ma."

"What you mean not today. Someone has got to put some sense to you. Good riddance to that dog in heat..."

"Mom! She's your grandchildren's mother."

Caleb's mom did not apologize. Caleb shook his head. "Ma!"

Mrs. Mitchell shook her head... "I didn't marry her. You did. That B wouldn't have been my choice for you, just like that ole bitty in Africa wasn't my choice, but you slid it right on in and got with child. You don't listen to me. You will get me one day. Boy!

All my grandkids are going to be away from me. Can't stand Tonya. I can understand an ocean of distance and culture. At least Katura makes Liana call and FaceTime with her grandmother. I can respect that. But Tonya, I can't stand her disrespectfulness. I put her in the same boat as your lying-ass uncles. May their soul be at unrest as they lay 6 feet under, and I hope their souls burn in hell. I pray to GOD they never sought his forgiveness. If God grants me the right to heaven, - and I see them there. I'm going to hell happily."

Caleb shook his head, but his visits with his mom, who spoke a lot about Tonya, were almost a therapy session. His mother spoke his inner mind, that he tried to pray away.

His mother looked at him. "Hmph. You know I'm telling you the truth, Caleb. Let her go. Holding on to her for the children's sake is going to be bad for you all. Your dad knows this. The children will learn. Look at me. You know, I wish I had never given birth to a boy. But as my son, love or no love, let it go for your own peace. I speak my truth. Not to hurt you but so you can endure. She is a virus that will kill you from the inside. Believe I know of that virus. Not in the sense of infidelity. But being abused and all you did was live. Satan comes to kill, steal, and destroy. He nearly got two of those things down pack with you. The last one is to DESTROY. He will do it slowly and painfully if you let him while you try to hold on to what you need to let God handle."

"But don't mind me. I see you. Keep at it, and I see your sin coming to you like the burning bush and Moses speaking with God. LET IT GO, and be Moses. Free from bondage. Or you will end up like Pharaoh in anguish, not heeding the call of God."

Caleb heard his mother, and deep down, he acknowledged what she said was right. But he couldn't let go of his own will. Caleb couldn't comprehend how not fighting for his children was the right thing to do. He loved them, and he wanted them to know it. He didn't want them to look at him like he looked at his mother.

Mrs. Mitchell became quiet as she turned away from her son, the sedative finally taking root in her system. Caleb watched his mother drift off to sleep as his father came back into the room after getting a cup of coffee.

"Caleb, your mom is right. You know I listened outside the room. The children will resent you and Tonya if you drag this out. It's been months now, and they are looking for peace and happiness any way they can get it. Even if that means accepting Tonya and Mike. Caleb Jr. has told me as such. He is an intelligent kid. They know you love them." Caleb looked at his dad and said nothing in response to the comment except, "I got to go."

He left his father as he didn't want to discuss his life anymore that day.

7

SET UP TO STEP UP

In despair, Caleb began attending City View Metropolitan Church. The same church his homeboy Reese had been begging him to visit. His Sunday morning visits led to his regular attendance at Saturday morning prayer. He spent many Saturday mornings praying to be healed and to recover all that the enemy had stolen from him. He was having a Job-like experience and desperately sought comfort but also answers.

Caleb thought of his father and the many nights he watched him go into a room- a room he could never step foot into. A room that his father would spend time in and come out like a brand-new man. He didn't understand the seeking of God. But since the night Tonya told him all that had occurred, He could hear his father in the prayer closet. It became clear to him.

Caleb knew he was up against so much in this life with his wife leaving. He prayed for her but felt she was beyond his thoughts, and it was a God project. His torment was thinking about his children and the man who would be an example before them. Caleb never imagined he would find himself married with children, only to be a divorcee and miss out on seeing his children growing up.

Caleb first found himself praying for God to save his marriage. To keep his family intact. But as time progressed, he saw Tonya getting farther and farther away from the woman of God he would need as he prayed. He had to let go.

It was a hard emotional pain that many women didn't understand; what they put a man through who loved his family. Caleb thought of how faithful he was to his wife. He did what he could and was working to get back on his feet. And just as it appeared he was about to make a turn for the better, he was being rewarded with a loss of family on a technicality of finance. He wanted to lash out, but he looked at his son, and he thought of his daughter.

One of the parents had to take the higher road, and he was the one carrying the mantle. Caleb studied the Book of Job in the Bible. He was losing it all. Nothing he did was of his own accord to merit this, but it was what life was giving him. Caleb knew God was in control, as he thought of the personality presented to him by Tonya.

God had his reasons, but for this cause, Caleb did not understand, so he had to get his house in order. It was not a house built of brick and mortar but a house that God gave to man when he blew into him, and he became a living soul.

Caleb had to seek God's face and become the house of prayer as one of his favorite Gospel artists sang.

He enjoyed Saturday prayer as only the pure in heart attended that time in the morning to pray. Sunday sometimes vexed his spirit as he saw Tonya's adulterous spirit running rapidly through the congregation of people in passing, and he had to ask God to shield him in order to get a word from the minister.

So, on some Sundays, he found himself at home. In his sacred place...He would walk into the second bedroom in his apartment. Lay out his prayer rug and submit himself to God. Knowing himself, he could not endure the pain of being unemployed, his children being raised by another man, and his ex-wife's infidelity. He wanted his peace back. He knew only God could do what he could not in his power. He cried out to God as only a man would in his quiet time away from the eyes of the world.

Caleb fasted from sun up to sundown and ate only at night. He had to denounce his flesh and allow the greatest within him to take over. His worship had to be of such. He thought of the night learning all that Tonya had done. He cringed on the inside. Never again would she have that effect on him, and never would a woman get the best of him like Eve. He would not denounce his humanity. He had to be diligent.

Upon visiting his mother during this time, she said very little to him. He saw her fear, as her spirit was tormented by past demons, and they knew he was not the Caleb a few months ago. His father loved what he saw in his son and continued to encourage Caleb to become the man God wanted him to be in the midst of all that he was enduring.

Caleb, totally consecrated to God, found himself being led by the spirit to give guidance to men and women who were dealing with life issues. He heard the voice quietly in his prayer time. For this cause, I have called you to ministry. Caleb didn't feel worthy as a divorced male, and he ran from the calling. Not wanting to be the setting example.

However, the calling came upon him stronger as he walked around the sanctuary. He prayed and praised God inwardly for his faith. He was confident that God would do exceedingly, abundantly above all he could ask. He just didn't think it would be at that exact moment, but he felt an unexplainable peace as he heard the voice of a woman praying. Her words spoke directly to his soul as she quoted Isaiah 54:4. His eyes found the person that his ears had already embraced. He silently made his request known to God.

Feeling led by God to put his thoughts on paper, he sat down on a pew, took out his Biblical study journal, and wrote a list of what he wanted in his next wife. He felt his flesh stir, and he rebuked it, but he felt a calling to be connected to the woman he saw. He questioned her entry into his life as it called to him in the flesh and in the spirit. He left her alone for a period. He ran from making contact personally, but he saw her from time to time. He didn't want to get involved with another woman with all that he was enduring.

As time went by, God settled his spirit as he fought for the custody of his children, only to lose the fight, and it devastated him. Caleb felt the anguish of knowing another man, the man who his wife had an affair with, would be raising his children. The inner spirit of God wrestled with the dark areas of his life. Caleb's agony strengthened his flesh, and he leaned into his own understanding.

Mike had made Caleb's life a living hell. The games Mike played on his employment status God worked for Caleb's good... but the lies Mike fed his children that he had to recant at every visit, Caleb was fed up. He kept praying until one day, his son broke down and cried and said I love you, dad. He knew his children couldn't keep up the brave face for him and Tonya. It was taking its toll, as his father had stated. Caleb knew he had to have a heart-to-heart with his children.

In this area of his life, concerning his children, Caleb was clear-minded and grounded within himself and with God. Caleb gave his children guidance for their life. He told them how much he loved them. He stressed how he never wanted them to experience a life of divorce or living without both parents being in their lives on a daily basis. The children listened as Caleb explained that sometimes decisions were made to make the best of a situation in the worst of times.

Looking at his son and daughter, Caleb began to speak life into their pain. "I want you two to be at peace. Remember what I am telling you today. I love you. I always want the best for you. Even if I'm not around, and if or when I miss the most important days of your everyday life. I want to be there for you, even when I can't. Remember this, you hear me. God said to train children in the way they should go, and they will not depart from it. A wise son heareth the instruction of his father," Caleb looked at his daughter, "You too..., and God further stated- to honor thy mother and thy father that thou days shall be long upon the land. The words I am giving you today is from the power that gave your mother and me the permission and granted us the gift to have you."

Caleb looked at them for understanding. They nodded and sat listening. Caleb continued. "The power that, from what I hear, Mike does not believe in. It is a power God himself requires me to tell you the truth. To raise you and give you good teachings so that you can become the best version of yourself and live a righteous life. Whatever you hear from others about me, remember my words and these passages when you hear something that makes you doubt my love for you, or someone says something about me that doesn't sit well with you. Never forget, it is the love of God and our love for God that guide us."

Caleb watched as a tear fell from each of his daughter's eyes, and he had to keep himself in check so as not to do the same. He worried about her, and it scared him the most... with her being away from him. Caleb asked God to protect her daily. He reached over and hugged her. "Daddy loves you, my girl."

His son, who did not want to be left out, stated excitedly, "I love you both!" Which brought a smile to all their faces, and Caleb continued to talk.

"I want you to take this inside your mind and seal it with your heart. REMEMBER this part no matter what... Okay...?" They both nodded.

"Like God, you can't see him, but he's there. He may not speak to you as I am speaking to you, but he left guidance for us in this book. You can read it from the internet or your phone if there isn't an actual book available. On your worst days, and you want to see me. Know, I am like God. I love you, but you can't see me. You will call me sometimes, and I cannot answer, but if I could be physically there in my power, I would. Remember this...

JOHN 15:9 -10 As the Father (God) hath loved me, so have I loved you: continue ye in my love. If ye keep my commandments, ye shall abide in my love; even as I have kept my Father's commandments, and abide in his love.

You know what I have taught you as truth. Your Grandfather has taught you. Remember my teachings because...I leave you with this when I am not around daily...

3 John 1:4: I have no greater joy than to hear that my children walk in truth.

This is not to be shared with or to anyone; it's for you and you alone... You hear me?" The children both nodded their heads and then hugged him. Caleb felt the peace of mind to let go and let GOD operate in the situation. He thought he had surrendered everything, but in this area concerning his children, it was harder to let go.

He prayed, asking God for discernment in the situation and peace for his children's sake. Caleb knew he and Mike would never see eye to eye with the whole situation. But by the Grace of God, Caleb was able to be a better man and find peace in allowing Mike to be in his children's life. But he put his foot down, letting Mike know that he would never relinquish his rights as their parent. Mike saw a power behind Caleb that he never thought was there, and he understood Tonya's wariness of her soon-to-be ex-husband. Mike accepted Caleb's terms, which were legally drawn and finalized before the divorce. Caleb finally let his children move from the state as he and Tonya waited the allotted time to finalize the divorce with custodial rights already in place.

Caleb thought he was in good standing to handle the situation until the plane took flight and the following weeks without seeing his children hit him. His inner spirit was in pain again, the silent issue that many women think men don't feel. Caleb shook his head as he watched social media clips of women bashing men, and he had enough info to squash all their thoughts with his life scenario. But instead...he went to church asking God for guidance and for HIS presence to help him.

During a particular service weeks after the children had left the state and a day that his flesh was being afflicted, Caleb saw the woman again, not far from him where he was sitting in the sanctuary. As he looked at her, he remembered his list about his next wife. Caleb thought *I am losing it all. Surely, God has a ram in the bush as he had for Abraham.*

However, his spiritual mind was telling him to pray more and to leave the woman alone. But Caleb's flesh was screaming louder with his inward pain pressing upon him. He began seeking other aspects of life other than God, which fed his flesh, making him spiritually weak as he heard her. She was praying a prayer that fed his inner being. He allowed his flesh to get the best of him- *Is she the* one? He questioned himself, as his inner being was conflicted. That can't be her! God, you gotta be kidding me?

Later that evening, Caleb visited a local market to pick up groceries for the upcoming week. This was the same market he had visited for years and had never seen the likes of her. *Could this be a divine moment, a sign that this is indeed an answer to his unspoken prayer request he made earlier?*

A gentle nudge begged him to silently pray. However, his flesh spoke louder, and his desire mixed with pain watched her...speaking into him. *She prayed a prayer that must be a connection.* Yet Caleb also heard a voice of reason... *Behave yourself, Man, Behave yourself!*

His mind screamed. Scrolling down the bread aisle, he unnoticeably scanned her from head to toe, and those yoga pants got him more excited than the prayers he had heard her say earlier that day. She was thicker than the woman he was usually attracted to, but he admitted that she was well-packaged. His lower member was reactive, and he silently prayed for deliverance from that moment on.

He looked to the left to distract his mind. He saw a package of hamburger buns and found himself gaining control until his eyes caught the hot dog buns. Shaking his head, he almost laughed out loud at the irony of it all. *Satan comes to kill, steal, and destroy.* Resonated within his mind. Then a scripture of *be fruitful and multiply* followed, with the *he who findeth a wife findeth a good thing*, and he was in trouble again with his flesh.

It was unavoidable. He was wanton, and as if driven, he had to satiate his desire in the best way possible to move forward with his day. The carts must have had an electromagnetic pull because he moved instantly toward hers and found a profound boldness to approach her. "Excuse me. Did I see you at City View church this morning?" His eyes remained solely on her, and he ignored the woman standing next to her cart.

"Yes, I was there."

Caleb wanted to move from behind his cart to shake her hand and introduce himself, but he was afraid that he would not be able to contain his excitement elsewhere.

"I thought you looked familiar. My name is Bethany, and this is my best friend, Necole."

Caleb greeted Necole while keeping his eyes on Bethany. "Nice to meet you, Bethany."

Caleb noticed that being in Bethany's presence seemed to have washed away all his agony. She was physically and spiritually beautiful and a breath of fresh air from the agony he had been feeling over the past several months. Not to mention the past several minutes. He watched her as she walked away, only to meet her again at the checkout line. He was happy she approached him. She was clearly interested in him as he was in her. Her mind clearly opened the doors of the church when she asked what service he attended. Her question fed his inner thoughts about his last prayer and sealed the idea of a divine connection.

When Caleb handed Bethany his business card, he felt a slight nudge to pray more and let her go. But he overrode it, thinking *the devil is a liar.* Bethany graciously accepted his card; he knew the connection was made for another meetup, and it just so happened to be at the next church service.

Caleb placed his groceries on the counter and his perishables in the refrigerator. His flesh was screaming for release as he drove off from the store, but he revisited his actions. He asked God to help him, and the next song in his playlist by Tamela Mann, Take Me to the King, made him ask God for forgiveness for not hearing and heeding the gentle nudge. As he stood looking out the window of his apartment, he looked toward the heavens and prayed.

Dear God,

I am a man. You made me this way. However, I know what true pain feels like. I don't want to keep making mistakes. You know I am weak and tired and looking for that other half. This body has needs. Help me keep a perspective on my actions. But I can't deny her prayers at church has my attention. Something I never had with my soon-to-be ex-wife. This woman, Bethany, with her interest in just knowing the service I attend, has mesmerized me. But God, you are the glory of my life. Keep me. You are my provider. I lay my issues at your feet. Order my steps.

Caleb walked away from his kitchen, feeling the pain of hunger in his stomach as his body was hungry for food. He needed his flesh to come under subjection to quelch the satiation of another hunger. Prayer dealt with it, while spiritual fasting helped to keep it that way.

"You still crying over that Gee Dee awful woman you called a wife?"

Caleb watched his mother as she took a step from her bed to a chair as he walked in to visit her.

"Hi, Mom," Caleb greeted while ignoring the question; she didn't forget.

"You heard me ask you a question, boy. How is that cow doing?"

"Mom, could you please..."

"Don't please me, boy. I can say what I want when I want, and you know she was a GEE DEE COW. You should have just gotten the milk and left that heifer in the field. She wasn't worth the beef you dealing with now. You sold her off yet. She ain't never gonna mount up to nothing but tough meat, something a man can't never chew on. I hear she done landed a rich fella. He aint shit, either. She's gonna wish she still had you, though, when he gets finished with her. Her rump is in for a rude awakening. Better get the money up for boarding school for the grandchildren. Hmph, life is interesting. You should have brought her around before you let that…"– she pointed her cane toward Caleb's trouser zipper.

"That's what's gonna get you this time around. Tonya was a cunning woman. The next one will be your undoing. Are you listening to me, boy?"

Caleb prayed as he heard his mother. She was his cold shower when it came to relationships. He just wanted to see his mother as it had been a while since he had just sat with her wide awake, knowing he was there and alert enough to talk to him.

"I know you done tuned me out, little Caleb. But mark my words."

Caleb's ears perked up. When his mother called him Little, it was her way of being endearing. He hated it but knew it was just her way.

"The next one could be your undoing if you aint careful. Mocha- brown and thick, boy, leave that one alone.

DO YOU HEAR ME? Leave her alone. There are some things in this life that you will connect with that feels good… and in the end, it will destroy you spiritually."

Caleb nodded as he thought of Bethany. *Surely my mom is not referring to Bethany?* He thought to himself. And he replayed her words. *Mocha brown and thick? Not sweet spiritual Bethany?*

Reminiscing a few weeks back when he met Bethany at the park, it was more than the magical kiss that they shared but the confirmation that she met everything on his list for his next wife. He was most impressed by the relationship she had with her father. This go-round, he wanted a woman who was different than Tonya in every way. Caleb gained insight into his parents' thoughts and considered his past situation with women.

He knew Tonya's experiences from childhood trauma fed into her brokenness due to not having a good father present in her life. But Caleb questioned his mother's thoughts, as Bethany came from a good family based on what he had learned.

What could be the problem with Bethany, other than the fact she wanted a child, and I honestly don't want anymore. I am sure that could be worked out. He looked at his mother as she sat in the chair and started to doze off. He heard her mumble in her sleep... "It's not always them. It's you," he wanted to dismiss his mother; she wasn't talking about Bethany.

Caleb didn't understand the gift of his mother. But the woman scared him sometimes. This was one of those times. *What's wrong with Bethany?* He asked himself. *Or me, for that matter.*

After seeing each other at church a couple of times and going out on a walking stroll, Caleb was genuinely interested in Bethany. His desire for her grew almost to an obsession, for in her presence, he felt peace and all his desires fulfilled. Spiritually, though, it became an inner war... and his mother's words became a reality.

Reese walked up to Caleb as he was deep in thought after a midweek service.

"Hey man, Caleb! Earth to Caleb..."

Caleb looked up, hearing his name, and finally saw his friend Reese.

"Hey, what's up, man."

"Obviously, it's not me saying hi to you, as you have ignored every attempt to gain your attention. What's got your thoughts? Since we know it wasn't Pastor Carlton's message tonight. I saw your looks when he talked about how some are called and others chosen. So, is it Tonya that's got you deep in thought as we wait for the parking lot to clear?"

Caleb smiled, "Nah, definitely not Tonya."

Reese looked at his friend intently, not overlooking Caleb's deliberate dismissal of the minister's sermon. Shaking his head, he knew of this Caleb back in the day before Tonya.

"Caleb. Hear me out. Get your stuff together before you step off into something else."

Caleb looked at Reese. "Not you, too, man."

"What do you mean not me too? Who is this woman that someone else is telling you the same thing?"

Caleb held up his hands. "It's not what you think. My mother said the same thing, and no one has ever met the woman yet. Heaven knows, I barely know her myself. I just find her interesting."

Reese looked around the church vestibule. Looking a little crazy, like comedic Eddie on stage.

"She goes here, Caleb? She has to because you just go to work, to the gym, to prayer service, and to every church service when the doors open. I mean, I don't see anything wrong with your choice of services for the church. But some of the women in this building could make Tonya look like Christ himself!"

Caleb busted out laughing at Reese's impression, which alerted a few women around them. And looking at their scowl at his outburst brought tears to Reese's eyes as he kept his laugh on the low, and he patted Caleb on the back.

"See man, see... Now I got to go and pray... to keep my soul. Those looks were death sentences."

Caleb busted out laughing some more. "Man, you should be his opening act. You got him down pat."

Reese looked at Caleb, feigning innocence, "I don't know what you're talking about. I'm just Jesus's little brother." Caleb shook his head as they walked out of the church to the nearly empty parking lot that had a traffic jam of cars only minutes ago.

Thinking about Reese and his mother's words, Caleb felt internally scolded, when he discovered Bethany's age- as their last meeting made him cringe. Caleb knew he was wrong to continue seeing her, knowing his divorce wasn't final. To add insult to injury, knowing her age made it worse. Bethany was a woman he should have met in his youth. Her values and wants in life did not align with his. She wanted children or a child should the relationship move forward. It was a near-deal breaker for him. But she was enticing. He knew walking away would be in their best interest. But she quieted the demons of his inner mind. Not to mention his flesh.

Damn...he cursed, asking for forgiveness as he reminisced

and heightened his arousal as he replayed burying himself within her warmth repeatedly. His mother's words came to him in full force... *It's not always them. It's you,* and he squashed the thought immediately.

Time passed, and several rendezvous occurred between him and Bethany before he met up with his friend Reese again at church. It was after service, and Reese saw him with Bethany on his arm.

To Caleb's surprise, Reese acknowledged that Bethany seemed nice. Reese even teased him about Bethany, making her blush as he commented on her being a beauty on his arm. Caleb was happy and was enjoying Reese's banter.

However, later in the week, Caleb received a surprise phone call from Reese. Caleb texted Reese after arriving home from church. He told Reese that Bethany knew of his situation because of his interrogation at the church.

Reese, being the friend that he was, disregarded Caleb's line of thought of blaming him for the situation. Reese lit into him. Laying all jokes aside and pleasantries from meeting Bethany, Reese was disappointed in Caleb.

"Caleb, what in the world are you doing, man? I mean, you do this- there- in the eyesight of GOD- you doing this...!?"

Caleb listened, feeling defeated, but did not rebut Reese's words.

"I told you to get your stuff straight before you move on to something else. What has gotten into you? You -better than this. I'm your friend. I got to tell you the truth. I always have and will... Your soul and life depend on it."

Caleb felt the weight of his decision. But he didn't want to let Bethany go. Her silent hurt was felt as she left him quietly after explaining his situation, and now, with his friend Reese, Caleb just wanted the pain to go away. He wanted a little peace by any means necessary, considering all that life was throwing at him. He felt her absence as he tried to contact her via text.

Bethany, call me. I can explain.
Bethany, I'm so sorry, don't be like this, I have reasons...

He also called her only to get her voicemail, and he repeated the exact verbiage. Only to get a message to give her time to think. One day, as he leaned back on his sofa, he received a call from her and was elated. They talked, and all was right in his world at the moment, even with demands that only made sense. But as time took its toll, Bethany wasn't enough to keep his inner demons at bay.

Needless to say, as time went on, Caleb continued to spend time with Bethany, and Reese had more choice words. But Caleb was not hearing any of it; he was getting his needs met. Going against his inner voice, he decided to enjoy this cake and eat it too for as long as he could, and he did just that. Loving Bethany is a story in its own right. Caleb knew he was wrong. But there was something about her, sweet, Bethany, mocha brown sister, that fed his inner being, and he dared to call it love.

Caleb realized in the world of dating, saying the words *The divorce is not final* is an invitation too many to pursue, and they were a demonic entity to a woman looking for her other half. Caleb knew he was playing with fire while entertaining Bethany. He knew he was the demonic entity, until his divorce was final.

8

CHANGE IS INEVITABLE

Caleb told Bethany about his mom and her health. He was surprised when she offered to visit his mother at his next visit. Caleb warned her about his mother's demeanor but felt a surge of confidence as Bethany just smiled and said God's grace was sufficient. He reached down and kissed her, and she returned it, deepening it to something more. It was hours later before they parted ways.

On Tuesday at 6 pm, they agreed to meet at the rehabilitation center. Mr. Mitchell met them in the lobby. Mr. Mitchell instantly liked Bethany but questioned Caleb on his divorce out of earshot of Bethany. Mr. Mitchell looked at his son and questioned his mental and spiritual fortitude when it came to the woman walking in front of them. Bethany paused as they reached the door to Mama Hazel's room. Mr. Mitchell knew this was not going to be a good visit, and he knew his wife, so he offered to go get coffee as they made introductions.

Caleb knew his father was staying clear of his mother's wrath should she not like Bethany.

Bethany watched Mr. Mitchell walk away. "Is everything okay?"

"Yeah, he just has a lot on his mind. Mom's health has taken its toll on him."

Mrs. Mitchell loved Bethany. She smiled, and the visit was pleasantly refreshing. Mr. Mitchell walked in to see Caleb watching Bethany comb his mother's hair and straightening up her room. Mrs. Mitchell looked at peace as she allowed Bethany to pamper her.

She smiled at Bethany's words of encouragement. But it was not lost on Mr. Mitchell or Caleb, Mrs. Mitchell's lack of interaction with Caleb. Mr. Mitchell took Bethany out to get dinner to give Caleb some alone time with his mother.

Bethany obliged as it was only to the cafeteria 5 floors down. Caleb watched his mother change as they left the room. Her eyes landed on Caleb. She quietly, in a death-still voice, said four words.

"You have become Tonya."

Not sure he heard her correctly, he looked at his mother. She stared at him sternly.

"Yeah, you heard me. WHOREDOM. And you fornicating with that sweet girl, making her an adulteress. May the depths of Hell swallow you whole for the ruin you will bring to her life. I told you to leave her alone! You've opened a box you can't return from. I warned you. You must go through.... The crossroads have been set, and your path has been chosen. Loving Bethany will change you. The duality of your spirit is lukewarm. God will spit you out."

Caleb stood still, and a cold feeling of hot anger and then numbness enveloped him. The pain of his past life hit him in full force, and he walked out of the room, slamming the door behind him. But not before hearing her words... and laughter.

"See, just like I thought.... You aint about shit. Never gonna be shit, either. Church or no church. Calling yourself a man of God. I see you. I know you, just like your grandfather and your lying, molesting uncles." Shaking her head, she repeated, 'Ain't shit' for about a minute. Looked at him and said, "You ain't doing right."

He heard her laughing as he walked out. "I told you... I told you, Caleb," she sang over and over again before the nurse came in and took her for a short exercise stroll.

Mr. Mitchell and Bethany walked into an empty room. Then, the nurse walked in with Mrs. Mitchell, repositioning her back in her bed. 15 minutes later, Caleb walked in with flowers from the flower shop. Mrs. Mitchell said nothing, as if the conversation with her son never took place. She looked at the flowers and then to Caleb.

Mrs. Mitchell knew they were the only excuse he could come up with for his absence and lapse in time. She smiled, but Caleb knew better as she mouthed a few words that only he could see. She watched them talk and then eventually fell asleep. Wanting to spend more time with Mrs. Mitchell, they all had dinner while his mother slept. Caleb kept his thoughts to himself. But his father knew better.

About a year passed by, and He and Bethany had their good and bad times. His divorce finally became final, but Caleb was still a mess on the inside. Feeling the effects of allowing his flesh to get the best of him, Caleb lashed out at the world around him. He lost his motivation to not only work but to get back to a functioning adult life. His mental instability was taking its toll. Knowing what he had to do and what his flesh desired tore him up on the inside. The peace he wished for was far from becoming a reality with his mindset.

Caleb cried out to God. He missed his children as their calls became less and less. His father prayed for him, and his mother kept it real. Bethany finally let him go for the sake of her own peace of mind.

A few months later, Caleb got a call from his father. He heard his father's voice crack, and he knew his mother had gone home to glory. Caleb felt his mother had cursed him when it came to Bethany's relationship. Mother gone and no Bethany during his grief, he questioned God. *Why am I left behind to deal with my sorrow and no solace for my soul?* The gentle nudge to pray pressed upon his spirit.

Caleb ignored it and, unlike Job, lashed out at God, which led to constant confessions to God for forgiveness, only to falter and fall. A Donnie McClurkin song became his anthem...*for a saint is just a sinner who fell down and got up...* This became his life and was all he could deal with as he thought of Bethany's absence and the aftermath of his mother's passing until something else that was held at bay emerged from Caleb.

Where are you, Bethany?

His mind screamed. *You just like her. That heifer left me at my lowest. All women are alike. As long as we men are here for your needs, you're good. The minute it comes to us, you bail.*

TO HELL WITH YOU ALL!

Caleb lashed out in a moment of agony as the one woman he needed to hear healing words to mend his inner trauma of wounds was no longer on this side of heaven. And with her death sealed, the final resolve to be something more than where he stood at the present moment. He realized he spent most of his life trying to prove his mother wrong.

Days after his mother's death, something deep within him snapped. Opening a deep wound of thought.

Women were no good.

Bethany included. His mother's words *Should of got the milk and let that heifer in the field,* resonated with him so much that his father had to walk away from his son's destructive, diabolical actions and thoughts. He went to his prayer room for his only child.

⁓ ❦ ⁓

Caleb went on a rampage of one-night stands and non-committal relationships due to his insatiable desire for Bethany. God intervened, knowing the heart of Caleb. God saw his hurt, knew his trauma, and understood his childhood and the mother he had given to his creation.

Caleb, during one service at church, while thinking somewhat clearly, sought God for guidance amidst his pain. He heard scriptures he had heard countless times before, but it slammed into his spirit as he stood in the aisle of the church alone in the back, away from most of the congregation, listening to every word of the pastor. It was like a fire burning and branding into his soul.

Pastor Carlton spoke... "God did not bring you through for you to be broken. His Grace is sufficient. Children of the Most High God. This word is for someone... I feel it in these prevalent times. Remember God's words. Jeremiah 29:11-15:

> *¹¹ For I know the thoughts that I think toward you, saith the Lord, thoughts of peace, and not of evil, to give you an expected end.*
>
> *¹² Then shall ye call upon me, and ye shall go and pray unto me, and I will hearken unto you.*

¹³ And ye shall seek me, and find me, when ye shall search for me with all your heart.

¹⁴ And I will be found of you, saith the Lord: and I will turn away your captivity, and I will gather you from all the nations, and from all the places whither I have driven you, saith the Lord, and I will bring you again into the place whence I caused you to be carried away captive.

¹⁵ Because ye have said, The Lord hath raised us up prophets in Babylon...

Dear Brother and Sisters, life may be hard right now. You may not see the light at the end of your turmoil. But know God is with you. He hears you. He knows what you need. Seek him. Ask him for his divine intervention. Consecrate your life... It is the righteous that find peace. Peace doesn't mean it will always be sunny, but even during the time of the storm, peace is still to let you know that in the midst of the storm, you can find comfort. We have to sacrifice. I know what you are thinking. I have already sacrificed so much in this life... with my living.

But how much did Christ sacrifice for our life? How much has anyone in our family sacrificed that you are able to stand here? It is by the Grace of God and your parents that you are living here today to hear this word...

In Jeremiah 1 and 5-10, there was a mandate from God for Jeremiah. Who are we to be or do differently? God said to Jeremiah- I am speaking these words to someone in here.

Can I get a witness?

This is your conversation with God. You know who you are. You know your calling. You will not rest until you walk the life meant for you. Letting go of the past.

Become who you were meant to be.
God knows ... He stated in his word...

Before I formed thee in the belly, I knew thee, and before thou camest forth out of the womb, I sanctified thee, and I ordained thee a prophet unto the nations.

6 Then said I, Ah, Lord God! behold, I cannot speak: for I am a child.

7 But the Lord said unto me, Say not, I am a child: for thou shalt go to all that I shall send thee, and whatsoever I command thee thou shalt speak.

8 Be not afraid of their faces: for I am with thee to deliver thee, saith the Lord.

9 Then the Lord put forth his hand and touched my mouth. And the Lord said unto me, Behold, I have put my words in thy mouth.

10 See, I have this day set thee over the nations and over the kingdoms, to root out, and to pull down, and to destroy, and to throw down, to build, and to plant."

⁓•⁓

Caleb's soul inwardly cried out to God, and his father, attending service that day, saw the presence of God dealing with Caleb. Mr. Mitchell walked up to his son- as Caleb let

GO and let God. Caleb Mitchell answered the call … and consecrated his life before God; as days and weeks passed by with much fasting and prayer, he found his balance and accepted his calling into Ministry.

Men's Retreat

Time took its course on Caleb. Even with his calling into the ministry, Bethany was a spiritual stronghold in his world. His desire for her did not wane during his time of mourning for his mother. But he was disappointed. He prayed as their world was a whirlwind of changes brought on due to his wants and Bethany's desires.

Loving Bethany was a story for Bethany to tell as Caleb moved forward to living his life without her. His new life beyond divorce was of a man seeking- a wife. Amazing how God operates.

Proverbs 18, the whole chapter ministered to his heart, and Caleb smiled as he read the scriptures God placed upon him. He frowned as he thought of the other Ministers who shared the pulpit with him, and Caleb harkened unto his inner voice to not judge... *for he who is without sin cast the first stone.* Caleb bowed his head, knowing what he would have to do. The white sheet would have to be lowered.

The men's retreat started off closed to women. The protest from the women of the church was not lost upon Caleb. But he requested the pastor to give him time with the men. Free of all restraints to be themselves with God. Letting go of being a father, provider, sustainer, protector, but just a man seeking GOD for guidance, with all that bombarded them with life. Giving them time alone to hear God clearly is sometimes lost when trying to meet the demands placed upon them. Many times, trying to hear God is taken for granted or lost in the day-to-day management of life.

This also encompasses the inner mental life that many women never take the time to see or try to understand or can understand when it comes to being a man. For real, a man understands that with all that he endures to keep life afloat, the woman's role is not to be belittled. Thus, he must take on this in stride with everything else placed upon him by the world standards of being a protector and provider. The world was placed upon his shoulders.

But when a woman knows her worth and his role, she compliments him, and she is his peace of mind in the midst of all that he endures. She is his rock of solace, a place of rest. If she embodies the virtue of Proverbs 31, he can do so much because of her.

Yet, he understands the power she yields should she turn against him and follow the worldly views against family and male understanding... In this manner, she has the power to be his greatness weakness, with the capability of taking away the very essence that makes him thrive. In this understanding, Caleb stood before the congregation and spoke.

"To the husbands who believe work money and not your time is going to keep her happy... wrong. To the men who believe giving her the looks of a well-dressed man in the gym and a beyond-figure salary and savings that make the average man cry will keep her happy.... wrong.

To the man who believes staying faithful and doing the will of God will keep her faithful... wrong. Nothing you do will keep a woman who doesn't want to be kept. Don't look down on these women, for if you are the man who believes it is your right to use, abuse, and take for granted the woman who wishes to be kept and she works to be the Proverbs 31 woman, and you squander the gift God gave... You are no better than the woman who doesn't want to be kept.

You look at me and say, well, you ain't married Minister Mitchell... We men have needs. I remember my first child's mother. Yes. A child out of wedlock more than 2000 miles away in another country across the ocean. I thought it was all about love, that love we call between a man and a woman upon meeting. But we split, and who is suffering the child. I thought it was the first wife who left with my two children, who were born in wedlock. I had the bank account and a gym membership.

She left me for someone shorter, not so built but wealthier, and the children you don't see with me are living in a different state. I stand before you as a fornicator, an adulterer. I used a woman to meet my needs, not knowing I was killing her spirit and sealing my eternity in hell. I had to ask God for forgiveness. I STILL DO.

My mother, God rest her soul, didn't want me. Told me so. But I can't blame her. It was her life. The life that God gave me to her to stand before you. To make this statement. You men who think it's okay to abuse a woman. I am a product of a warped woman's mindset. She never healed entirely from the emotional and mental abuse of molestation.

My father is God's blessing in my life. Showed me what love is for a woman. In spite of her brokenness, he loved my mother through it all. Married her broken, and I knew he could have done better with a different wife. But he saw my mother and loved her, and she loved him the best way she could and gave him a son. It hurt her to see me grow up, but she was a woman who wanted to be kept by my father and my father alone.

She sacrificed her inner fears and birthed into the world a son who stands before you. We have to do better as men. Our women are looking for us to stand. But it is hard on us, too. I understand this. But to whom much is given, much is required. I know we have men in the church abusing, using, and not following the righteousness of GOD in their actions. I am coming out of this pulpit, and I am going before the altar. Not completely clean.

I have my faults. But God knows my heart. Sees my desires. He knows me better than I know myself. I am giving him my life to be my leader, teacher, and guide. I am just a man seeking after GOD to have a pure relationship with MY CREATOR. This is an altar call where you must come to GOD of your own accord. Seeking for HIS divine presence to find you and give you what you need most."

Caleb put his mic down and walked off the pulpit. Turned his back to the congregation and yelled, FATHER FORGIVE ME, FOR I KNOW NOT WHAT I DO. FIND FAVOR, TO

HEAR MY PLEA. And Caleb fell face down in tears before the spiritual throne of God.

This was just the beginning for Caleb to let go of his past. God knew his child; even though he was still plagued with his inner demons, Caleb had to come to terms with his life purpose. As his mother stated, the path was chosen he had to walk through.

9

THE STEP UP

She sat as a lone woman who had heard about the men's retreat from a fellow colleague. As she sat at her table, she listened to the talk of the cafeteria, not only amongst single folk like herself but her married coworkers as well who, unlike her, attended the most prominent mega-church in the city. Her ears perked up as one lady spoke at a table behind her.

"Girl, I have never seen my man like he was when he came home. I mean, the man came in and hugged me so tight and told me to go sit down; he got dinner. I was like, babe, I got dinner almost ready. He was like okay, go get the children, and I will handle the rest."

All the ladies at the table looked at her knowingly as they had their own experiences. As soon as one told their thoughts, another was soon to follow until one lady got interrupted and didn't care when she found out who the story was about.

"I hear you, but that ain't got nothing on what I heard...." The second speaker was interrupted by another co-worker. "Sorry, but Nah, girls. I have gots to tell y'all this..."

The lone woman listening almost gave herself away from listening; she almost laughed as the conversation went from uber-professional to a girls' night out conversation.

"Nah, girl, see I hearrrd, I heard that woman in the HR department, you know, the one I'm talking about. We need to go and pray with her. I mean, real-LEEE pray for her. Her usual enticing antics with several of the married men in the office ain't working."

Some of the ladies nodded their heads, and others were like what?! Tells us more. "Well, I heard that in the last few days, she has been politely put in her place."

"Yeah, I heard about that, and I saw her wiping her eyes in the ladies' room this morning. I know she was crying, and rumor has it she is now looking for a new job."

"But we can't let her go like that. If those men got their life together. The least we good Christian women can do is try to get her to understand her ways." An older woman at the table interjected.

"Yeah, I think that is a good idea. I heard her crying in the bathroom the other day, too. I think she doesn't know what else to do. Plus, rumor has it that one of the department managers is her child's father, and he is married with children."

"Oh, No! Not Pauline's husband?"

"Yep, one and the same. I'm not sure if it is true... but I do know he has been trying to talk to her and get her to change her ways."

"Oh well... You know how Pauline is going to handle it. I just don't know if the girl can handle Pauline."

"I know what you mean. Knowing Pauline, she would take the woman in since she is of a certain faith. I'm surprised her husband hadn't suggested it."

"I believe he did, but the woman didn't want to stop playing the field. But she might now."

"We will see."

The ladies turned their heads as they saw movement from the entrance of the cafeteria.

"Oh, there she is," one lady at the table stated. "Oh, my look at her today."

The normal provocatively dressed woman donned a demure, loose-fitting pantsuit that complimented her form femininely. They watched as the department manager walked up to a woman and quietly talked to her. She bowed her head in submission to his words, then looked up with gratitude and smiled. He walked away as another woman walked in modest attire, adorning a hijab. The modestly attired woman smiled and linked her arms with the woman as they walked out behind the man toward the entrance of the building.

"See, I told you Pauline was no one to play with. I don't know much about that faith. But one thing I know for the ones who do right they honor family life- not wanting nor leaving a woman to be left to whoredom or their children raised without family structure. Pauline and her husband were born Somali and have been in America for more than a decade now."

"Do you think she will convert?" One person in the group asked. They all paused in thought, shrugged their shoulders, and then another topic emerged.

"I heard the minister that night is like OMG. Fine!"

"Stop it. I can't be hearing you talk like that. I have a man to go home to."

"Girl, What God created, I can say THANK YOU, Jesus, for making them look pleasing to the eye. It's not like I'm lusting- ALL I said WAS he's FINE! Geesh." Everyone laughed.

"Did anyone get his name?"

"My youngest son, who came home from college to attend the men's retreat, was talking to one of his friends one night. They kept saying Minister M., that is all I got."

"Minister M. hmm."

"I wonder what's his story? And what did he say to all those men who attended the retreat? They are walking around here like the wrath of God is at their heel. I mean, I have never seen men be like this."

"I know what you mean."

"Now, we are enjoying this, but the women who don't know their worth are at a loss. The brothers are looking but not biting. Cordial but not over-friendly, and the women around here are like, what is going on...?"

"Pauline's story is a rarity. I heard one girl went loco on one of the guys during lunch last week. She threatened to tell his wife everything. She thought she had the upper hand.

Well, surprisingly, the man looked at her crestfallen and said I told her last night, and I am looking at the possibility of divorce. What more can you do to me. He walked away with her standing there looking stupid."

"Yeah, the stories about the men are getting really interesting. But what catches my ultimate attention- Is all these wives coming in here with lunch boxes for their men. I mean, like, what did these men do when they got home?" They all laughed as they discussed their own husband's reactions.

"Girl, if this is the treatment I can get if I do... Shoot. I am on it like white on rice.... Love me some, him." They all laughed.

"I found him." One lady stated she had been playing on her phone. "Who?"

"The minister who spoke that night. Look right here on the church website. Minister Caleb Mitchell."

"Not the Caleb Mitchell I know." One of the girls at the table stated. "He and I went to the same college. I heard he married some woman, had two children, and then divorced. Rumor has it she cheated on him at his lowest point in life."

The women at the table listened. "From some of my male friends who know of him said he took it hard. Then he went into the Ministry."

"Well, if he went through all that and is speaking truth to power, his ministry is GOD Ordained. Our world needs an overhaul, a divine intervention in family and married life. Especially with infidelity, divorce, and this so-called alternative lifestyle- DL being at an all-time high, it's like anything goes these days without accountability of righteousness regarding marriage." They all nodded, not saying anything more.

The lone woman took in everything but missed hearing the name of the male as she left to dispose of her tray and eating utensils. A department head with a few sub-department heads called to her. Hey ... did you finish that report? Acknowledging them with a yes and then looked back at the table of women and smiled. She knew a thing or two about life after divorce. The minister sounded interesting. Something she hadn't heard herself say about a man in a long time. Religious... hmm, something she grew up with but never took to in her adult life. A tug came upon her heart. Why, she didn't know, as she followed her colleagues to give them the completed report on her desk.

After several months of being on a Christians Dating with Purpose site, Caleb received a message from a beautiful bronze model-looking woman in Atlanta.

> *Hello handsome. I read your profile,*
> *and I became very intrigued. And I am interested in*
> *getting to know you. If my profile is appealing to*
> *you, I would love to hear from you.*

Caleb clicked on her profile and was amazed at not only her beauty but also her intellect. She had a master's in accounting and attended an Ivy League institution. She had been married once like him. She had grown twin daughters in college. *Hello, how are you? I can tell from your profile that you are intelligent and beautiful.*

Within a few moments, Kacey Sims responded. *Thank you so much. So, tell me a little more about you. I read that you live in Huntsville, been married once, three children, and work for the government.*

Yep. I am divorced. I have a daughter in Africa when I worked internationally and a daughter and son from my ex-wife.

How long have you been divorced?

3 years. What about you? How long have you been divorced?

7 years.

Okay. May I ask why?

*To make a long story short,
I'll just say we grew apart. Yours?*

Adultery.

Wow! You or her?

She did.

Kacey let out a deep sigh of relief
as she thought he had cheated on his ex-wife.
I'm sorry to hear that. Women cheat just as much as men.

Maybe even more. Lol

Maybe. Caleb wrote.
So, you know I want to know more about your divorce, right?

Lol. Okay, I got married very young. Right after college to a man who was fifteen years older than me. He paid my way through graduate school. We built a nice family together with our twin daughters. He was a great man. As I grew into womanhood, we grew further and further apart.

Oh wow! Did you love him?

In the beginning, I did. I was just too young, and he had way more experience than me and he was settled. There was so much I didn't know about myself. I love him for giving me two beautiful daughters and for understanding in the end that I needed to be my own person. Which led to our mutual divorce. He's remarried now.

Gotcha. I understand. Tell me something else about you. Caleb requested.

I am originally from New Orleans. My parents are deceased, but my siblings are still there. Are you initially from Huntsville, before your travels?

Yes, I am. My mother passed away a couple years ago, and my aunt, who was like my second mother recently, died a few months ago.

Oh no! I'm sorry to hear that. How are you holding up?
I know it can be tough.

Honestly, it has been hard. It feels like I am all alone.

I'm here for you.

Oh really? Lol

Yeah, I felt the same way when my parents died.
I know what you are going through, and sometimes,
you just need to know someone is there to listen to how you
feel.

That's true.

Here is my number. 404-555-0101.
Call me anytime you need to talk.

Cool. Thanks.

Caleb flopped back on his pillow, looking at Kacey's pictures on her profile. Mesmerizing over her beauty and the things that they had in common. She was only a few years younger than him, and he thought that a woman closer in age and having similar life experiences would be a better fit for him.

He marveled at how the conversation flowed and how empathetic she was to the loss he was experiencing. Desiring not to move too fast, Caleb decided to just communicate with her via the dating site for about three weeks before actually speaking with her on the phone.

Kacey never insisted on more. She truly became a listening ear and shoulder for him to lean on. Caleb was immensely enjoying the pressure-free way of getting to know Kacey, and he began to feel safe enough to move a step further.

"Hello." A light, sexy, yet confused voice answered the phone.

"Hello, Kacey." Caleb mustered up the deepest and sexy voice to respond.

"Yes, this is she. Who is speaking?"

"My name is Caleb."

Kacey let out an unbelievable laugh. "Oh my gosh, Caleb! It is good to finally hear your voice. How are you?"

Caleb returned the laugh as he knew it would be a surprise. "I'm good. How are you, madam?"

"I...am...good. Yeah, I am great."

"Are you sure?"

"Of course I am. Your call has really made my day."

"That's great to hear." Caleb chuckled. "Is this a good time to talk?"

"Sure. I am just home relaxing."

"Same here. Just finishing eating."

"Did you cook mister?"

"Actually, I did. I eat out too much, so I decided to cook. Did you cook today?"

"Well, not today. I picked up a smoothie on the way home from work."

"That's it?"

"Yeah, I'm trying to get back to high school fine."

"I hear ya, but you still got it if you ask me."

"Awe, that's sweet of you."

"It's the truth."

"Well, thank you." Kacey acknowledged his compliment even though she was unsatisfied with her weight gain in the last few months. She knew she had been stress eating and needed to get off the weight she had put on.

"So, I was thinking about coming to Huntsville soon to meet Mister Caleb."

"Sweetheart, I am a real man. I couldn't let you come here on our first meeting."

"I don't mind driving. It will be nice to get away for a weekend."

"I hear you. But if you don't mind, I would like to do the honors of coming to your city first." Caleb stated.

"I don't mind at all. Did you have a date in mind?"

"Let me check my calendar for the week after next, and I'll text you to see if that works."

"Sounds good."

"Great. I'm headed to the gym now, but may I call you later?"

"Of course. Talk to you soon."

After agreeing to visit Kacey first, Caleb kept thinking that three and a half hours was a long drive. He decided to be more strategic in his conversations with her to determine if the trip was really worth more than the beauty she possessed.

Caleb was a very frugal person who didn't like wasting money. He knew it was time to get down to some important questions to see if she fit the bill. Caleb ripped up his list of what he wanted in a woman after meeting Bethany since she matched his list ninety percent. Caleb thought, *okay, Kacey, let's see about you...*

Needing his next relationship to be better than the ones before, he did some research. He came across a list of questions that should be answered before the first date. Caleb was elated as he read the comments from several relationship pages on social media and how well they worked. He wrote down every single one of the questions with the highest ratings and planned to record Kacey's answers when he talked to her again.

The next evening, after getting settled in from work and the gym, Caleb decided to give Kacey a call. The phone rang three times before he heard her sing a sweet "Hello, Caleb."

He let out a manly laugh as he responded hello back.

"How was your day?"

Kacey smiled her response through the phone, "It was great. How was your day?"

"It was good. I'm not disturbing you, am I?"

"Not at all. Never!"

"Cool." Caleb paused before jumping into his list of questions. "I want to ask you some more questions to get to know you a little better tonight, if you don't mind?"

"Of course. I am glad that you are interested in getting to know me." She laughed.

"Yes, I have enjoyed talking to you and wanted to give a bit more purpose to our conversations."

Wow! Kacey admired how Caleb was taking the lead. "I like that," she responded.

"Cool. Let me know if it becomes overwhelming." Caleb took out his pen and notepad to write down her responses. "I know you have adult twin daughters. Do you want to have any more children?"

"Oh God, No. Well, I guess if my spouse wanted to, I couldn't be selfish. Do you?"

"Not at all. I thought I was open to it, but I don't wish to start over."

"I feel you on that. I wish to enjoy all of my next boo and travel."

"Nice." Caleb jotted down her response before asking his next question. "What is your relationship like with your daughters' father?"

"It's good. We are friends. We just realized that we were better friends than spouses. Do you and your ex-wife have an amicable relationship now?"

"I don't really talk to her unless it is about the kids."

"I see. Do you think you are over that hurt?"

"Yep!"

There was that awkward silence for what seemed like an eternity until Kacey calmly replied, "That's good." Her response broke the ice and made Caleb comfortable to continue with his questions. Kacey heard his response, but something told her to be patient.

"Do you prefer dating multiple people or getting to know one person at a time?"

"Until I am in a committed relationship, I will get to know multiple people, but it is pretty dry over here."

"No way. I know men are knocking each other out of the way to get to you."

Kacey laughed, wishing it was true, but she played into Caleb's comment.

"Well, maybe just a few. But I do have my standards. Which may deter most."

"There's the truth," Caleb jokingly responded.

Kacey, not wanting to be in the dark about him, said, "Your turn. What is your dating style?"

Caleb knew what was genuinely true and how he was feeling at the moment. He spoke from his ideology rather than his reality. "I usually try to get to know one woman at a time."

"Unbelievable."

"Why?"

"You are just unbelievable. That is not the concept from most of the men I meet."

"I'm not your average man." Caleb chuckled.

"I'm learning," Kacey chuckled along with him.

"So, is there anyone that might feel like you are in a relationship with them?" Caleb asked.

"Not at all. I meet up with an old friend for dinner from time to time, but it is strictly platonic."

"Gotcha. So, if we started dating, would you tell him about me?"

"Of course." The truth was she had already mentioned Caleb to him.

"Okay...okay." Changing the subject, Caleb asked her about her spiritual beliefs.

"Do you believe in God?"

"Well, I believe there is a God. I was raised in the church, but I haven't been active in years. I need to find me a church."

"I understand. I had a period of time when I was not active either."

"Really! I was waiting on the judgment."

"No way, I can't judge anyone. I am still growing, and I'm definitely not perfect."

"That's a relief."

Caleb removed the phone from his ear as a beep interrupted his conversation. Even though he was trying to get over his previous love affair, he always made himself available when he saw Bethany calling, especially after reconnecting with her.

Refusing to give too much information too soon, Caleb lied about the incoming call. "Hey, my daughter is calling. May I call you back another time?"

"Of course."

Ending the call, Caleb clicked over to Bethany's call. He answered with a cheery "Hello."

"Hey, Caleb. What are you up to?"

"Nothing much. How are you doing?"

"I'm okay. Do you want to come over and watch a movie with me?"

"Sure!"

"Great! I have the wine."

Caleb laughed as his heart smiled, "See you in a few."

Caleb couldn't figure out what it was about Bethany. He had no trouble getting over any woman from his past, but he could not move past Bethany. He was there any time she called. He just loved to be in her presence. He thought of his new list and recognized he didn't want to ask Bethany any of the hardcore questions he required from Kacey.

He dismissed the answer to why... He knew he was biased when it came to Bethany... His feelings for her were on a different level. *How can you hate the person you love?* Caleb thought. Bethany was everything he wanted in a wife. Smart and spiritual, and she has a great relationship with her family. Bethany was a classic lady in the streets and a freak in the sheets. Even though he was madly in love with her, he could not shake the fact that she left him like his ex-wife Tonya.

With a mixture of anger and love, Caleb made an inner vow that they could only be friends with benefits. But their intimacy grew stronger than his flesh could control. He sometimes questioned his feelings about her...

His spiritual inner guide beckoned him to think more of why he felt the way that he did.

Appearing at her home, Caleb entered Bethany's place and got comfortable. She poured them a glass of wine and then flopped on the sofa beside him.

"Cheers!" They both said as they moved their glasses to tap each other's.

"So, what's been going on with you mister? What's new?"

"Nothing, really. Just working." Caleb stated before asking her a question that he asked from time to time.

"So, who are you talking to?"

"Huh?" Bethany looked at him, hoping she had heard him wrong.

"You heard me; who have you been talking to? Don't think I haven't forgotten about Valentine's Day and you not responded to my text. I haven't heard from you in about a month or so, don't lie." Caleb stated as he took a sip of wine and waited.

"Well, I was kicking with this guy I met game night at the main event."

"What happened?" Caleb asked as he began to get frustrated with thoughts of Bethany using him when things didn't work out with other men.

"He has a lot of issues similar to when I met you, and I just could not go down that road again."

"What do you mean?"

"He is not fully divorced and has financial issues."

Caleb was perturbed hearing she was comparing a guy she barely knew to him, but he kept his composure as Bethany became emotional.

"What's wrong with me? Why do I continue to attract men that are unavailable to me? Why does it have to be so hard?"

Caleb used his thumb and traced her tears. "Bethany, there is nothing wrong with you. Life is just complicated at times."

"Yeah, I know," Bethany whimpered. "Anyways, back to the original question. Who have you been talking to?"

Caleb contemplated telling Bethany the truth. He weighed the pros and cons and decided telling her could possibly initiate a type of jealousy that would cause Bethany to give them another chance.

"I have been chatting with this one woman."

"I knew it!"

"It's not like that. She lives in Atlanta, and we have just been talking on the phone."

"Cool. Let me see a picture of her."

Caleb pulled out his phone and scrolled to find his favorite picture of Kacey from the site.

"Oh, she's cute, Caleb." Bethany continued to pry, "Do you like her?"

This was not the response he desired. Was Bethany really over him? Caleb was definitely not over her and secretly hoped he could prove his love for her by remaining friends. Although his mother's words, stating that he should leave her alone, kept badgering him. For his mother's words had become a reality. Looking at Bethany and thinking of his past relationships and actions made him cautious spiritually. But his fleshly desire for her was like an addiction.

Reese considered Bethany as his demon's calling card to derail him. Caleb heard him, but he never prayed for her to be removed from his life. Reese kept repeating the idea as he was looking up to Caleb as the minister. Taking in the question from Bethany, he dismissed Reese and his mother; he thought of Kacey and superficially gave Bethany an answer. This in itself spoke volumes to his spirit, but his flesh overrode the thought.

"She is pretty cool. Just taking my time to get to know her."

"Tell me about her."

"She is around my age, married once with two daughters, and she is an accountant."

"That's wonderful. I really like her for you."

"Really?" Caleb stated with a question. He was not expecting that response from Bethany. He was a little disappointed that she showed no signs of jealousy. Maybe she really wanted to be friends after all they had been through.

"We will see," Caleb responded as he asked her what movie they were going to watch, ending the conversation. If confusion was a person, it was definitely these two.

They were comfortable on the sofa, cuddled up, pretending to watch the movie as Caleb caressed her arm that trailed inward, feeling the fullness of her chest. He then reached under her shirt, feeling her mocha skin, as Bethany placed her backside in just the right spot to amplify his already arousing parts. His hands moved from the softness of her chest back to her arms to the curves of her backside. Bethany began to moan as she took his hand and led it to the places, she wanted to be touched the most.

"Baby, you are wet," he whispered in her ear. "Is this for......?"

"Yeah," she moaned.

Caleb let his flesh get the best of him as he took pleasure in all that she had to offer without restraint. Bethany called out his name as he drove into her. She met him with a full embrace repeatedly until she quivered, and they shuddered both with a sounding release. Kacey became a fleeting thought, as Caleb held Bethany to him and they rested in each other's arms.

In these transcendental moments, Bethany fed him; his heart longed for her in more ways than she was willing to give. He knew it was his fault, her distrust of him. He was aware of what was required of him, but his pain would not let him see it. With an overwhelming feeling of care, he kissed her gently. Cherishing her into a second round of intimate connections. It was only in these moments that he felt Bethany's love for him.

Caleb slowly laid Bethany on her back and pursued to make love to her as if it were to be his last time. Sensually taking and giving until they both lay spent on Bethany's living room floor.

❦

Upon returning home, Caleb felt utterly alone and longed for something more. A deep, intense feeling of emptiness engulfed him. For some reason, his mind wandered to Kacey... and the up-and-coming trip to visit her. His spirit gave a little nudge, and he walked into his prayer room. Not seeking forgiveness as his past actions called to him with an urgency with Bethany. Their chemistry was strong and passionately intense. So, he could only ask God to help him do what he could not do on his own- let Bethany go.

10

HE WHO SEEKETH

Caleb's drive to Atlanta to meet Kacey for the first time was a smooth ride until he arrived in the city. The midtown traffic was stressful as he tried to navigate Peachtree Road. One wrong turn almost landed him in Gwinnett, which caused his arrival to be 45 minutes later than scheduled, but just in time for their reservation not to be canceled.

Kacey waited for him in the foyer, and when he arrived, she finally exhaled, pleased that she had not been ghosted or, even worse, catfished. He appeased her eyes more than the profile pictures. Caleb greeted her with I'm sorry to keep you waiting. Kacey stood and gave him a reassuring smile that he was worth the wait.

"Atlanta traffic is very unpredictable. It is okay," she said.

"Tell me about it. I don't know how you do it."

Caleb smiled brilliantly yet thoughtfully. Kacey smiled

knowingly... "You get used to it." Caleb heard her, but his eyes found her more appealing than he had thought. His voice and actions were taken over by something he couldn't understand or explain.

"Forgive my manners. You look stunning." Finding her hand in his, he gave her a spin. Kacey giggled as she was happy that the black shimmer long-sleeve romper, her 7-inch red bottom, and lightly applied lipstick sealed the deal.

"Thank you so much. You clean up very nicely yourself." Caleb felt a little something within as she acknowledged that she found him attractive.

"Your table is this way." The hostess interrupted their first in-person interaction as she escorted them to their table. "After you," Caleb stated, extending his arm for her to precede him.

Walking behind her he was awarded the opportunity to look at her. She was shorter than most women he became involved with, but her heels made up for the height difference. He watched her body sway, and he noticed he was very much attracted to her beyond their conversations. However, a part of him remained behind a wall.

The hostess escorted them to their table in the dim light room with a melody of classical music flowing from the pianist just a few feet away. Caleb tried to stop thinking about Bethany as he looked around the restaurant. *This is a place I would love to experience with Bethany*, he thought.

Due to his financial struggles when they first met, he was unable to take Bethany out on nice dates. He felt a little guilty about the investment he was making in getting to know Kacey. He questioned why he hadn't taken the measures to invest in Bethany? Before the truth found itself at the forefront of his mind, he pushed the thoughts aside. Caleb focused on the reason he made the drive and enjoyed the good food and conversation with his date.

After a little small talk, Kacey began to pry into his past relationships. She had not asked about any prior relationships other than his marriage in their previous phone conversations. Caleb, a little concerned and his radar up in regards to being questioned, looked at her, thinking in his mind, *Why now... and What was this all about?*

"So, when was your last serious relationship?"

Caleb remembered all the questions he had for her. He remembered her openness to answer. His inner mind thought *she was not being unreasonable.* Smiling within himself. She was proving to be the same on the phone and in person. This tugged at his inner strings, and for some reason, out of the abundance of his heart, which surprised him, he was ready to talk about Bethany. He knew this could ruin his potential progress with Kacey, but he didn't care. He considered himself an honest man, and for some reason, she made him want to open up and talk.

"My last serious relationship ended about a year ago."

"How long were you all together?"

"We were off and on for about two years."

"May I ask what happened?"

"I was going through a lot at the time with my ex-wife, and business was not doing well. It became too much for her."

"So, she left you?"

"Yeah, it's all good. We are still friends."

Kacey seemed to be unbothered by what would appear to be red flags to any other woman.

"Well, I would never leave you. I am serious about my relationships, Caleb."

Caleb chuckled, "For better or worse, huh?"

Kacey smiled and responded, "Indeed."

Caleb admired the fact that Kacey was not the jealous type and didn't mind if he had female friends. Her words soothed his heart in a way that Bethany did not. Deep down, he longed for loyalty and had yet to have found it in any relationship before. That is the one thing that Bethany was missing and that Kacey was offering.

The night ended like two friends who had not seen each other in a long time. Hugs and laughter. Caleb politely walked Kacey to her car, and as a perfect gentleman does, he opened her door and asked her to let him know when she got home.

Caleb checked into his hotel room alone and caught the last of the Heat and Lakers game.

Hey, good-looking.

Caleb read as he glanced at his phone after hearing the notification sound of a message waiting.

Hey Beautiful. Have you made it home?

I have. I really enjoyed meeting you. Thank you for driving all this way.

No, thank you. I wanted to meet you in person, and I am glad I did.

Me too, and next time, it's on me...

Caleb sent a happy face emoji as he was not ready to state otherwise. Kacey responded

Wyd.

Watching the game.

Heat and the Lakers?

Yeah, how did you know?

It was a guess. I am watching it, too.

Oh, I didn't know you liked basketball.

It is my favorite sport to watch.

Caleb was excited that Kacey was into sports just as much as he was. He knew any woman in his life had to accept the fact that he was a sports fanatic. He was not compromising on that.

Caleb and Kacey spent the next hour texting about the game, and the laughter from earlier that night continued. His interest in Kacey was definitely increasing but she had been solid from day one, and Caleb's inner spirit recognized it.

Caleb and Kacey were not officially a couple, but they began to talk on a regular basis. Kacey had made her way to Huntsville to see Caleb staying at a hotel and having rendezvous dates. Eventually, after Caleb became more financially stable, she stayed at his place for the weekend.

6 months later

Kacey drove up to his complex. A new apartment complex in the MidCity district that Caleb had moved into just a few months ago. Much like Atlanta's Atlantic Station, his residential living was incorporated within walking distance of shops and restaurants. She made herself known to the gated security. Caleb chimed her in and gave her directions to meet him at the private parking deck. Caleb helped her with her bags as they walked through an enclosed breezeway to the residential area.

Kacey took in the scene around her. A beautiful courtyard with a covered area and a partially enclosed pool area was to her right. Off the side of it was a restaurant bar. Clearly created for the sunbathing enthusiast. Her head was on a swivel as she glimpsed different cuisine restaurants just walking distance from the extended courtyard that traveled the length of the residential area above. Looking back at the door that hid the parking deck from this area, she was impressed with the design.

"Caleb, you must never want to leave home literally with all these amenities."

Looking at all she was taking in. Caleb was secure in his living. Happy to be where he was. It was needed after losing so much. But it wasn't land. It wasn't a home. It was a bachelor pad. Thinking about his age, in a place he never thought he'd be. Being open and honest with her was easy as he made his thoughts known. Kacey nodded, but she lightened the mood.

"It's a blessing, Caleb. There is so much to do, and all you have to do is walk out, and it's all at your fingertips. Life is meant to be lived. This is living on this side of singlehood."

Caleb looked at her as she spoke a truth he was still trying to accept. Bethany came to mind as they walked to his residential home, and he dismissed the thought.

"Welcome to my humble abode."

Kacey laughed, thinking about the authentic upscale restaurant that she had only heard about and saw nestled in the far corner at the end of the street below the breezeway they just traveled.

"Caleb, this is far from humbled."

They both laughed as they walked into his 3-bedroom masculine 1500 square foot décor apartment. Kacey took in the ambiance. Clean and modern, dark cherry woods mixed with dark expresso and light beige. It was cozy and romantic, with straight-lined furniture and curved accented pieces that gave a welcoming look.

Caleb took her things into the room he decorated for his daughters should they visit. A green and white room with splashes of lavender. Kacey looked into the room where he placed her bags and smiled inwardly, thinking *Gentleman Caleb.* She knew their relationship was still in the process of getting to know each other, although she wanted more. Caleb was proving to be just what she needed and wanted in a man. His home gave more insight into his life.

Kacey had a flashback of years of taking care of home life and catering to her husband. As she looked around, she had to ask a question. "So, you keep this place like this all the time, or does Ms. Ester come and clean it for you two days a week?"

Caleb laughed as he thought of Tonya for the first time in a long time and was able to find humor. "No Esters. This is me... Now, my room may be a little different."

"Where is it?" She questioned with laughter in her voice.

"Oh, just like a woman got to know the man's habits." Caleb stated, smiling at her look of investigating and finding humor in it all.

She looked at him. "With all the cooking and cleaning (she mocked in a Madea voice) I did, I have to know."

Caleb raised an eyebrow. Pointing to her, "You cooked, cleaned, and maintained a job while married?"

"Yes... We women do exist. I had a little help on the weekends, but not much. As the girls got older, they had to fend for themselves, as they had to learn, but yes... I took care of my family."

Caleb nodded and walked her to his room with a disclaimer. Not sure what to expect with his adamant disclaimer, Kacey hit him jokingly on his shoulder as she peeked in. A load of clothes was folded neatly on the bed with neatly organized drawers open to receive them, along with a few items hanging off the side of a chair waiting to be hung up. She looked across the room. After mentioning his room was not bad, she asked, a little excited... "Is that a walk-in closet?"

Caleb laughed. Of all the things he was thinking about with his room. Kacey got excited about his closet. It was his favorite feature in the room.

"Yes it...." He didn't get a chance to get the words out as Kacey walked past everything to the closet, which was a room in itself. It was decorated immaculately with his shoes and suits, shirts and ties. She spun around in it and looked at him. "I want one of these..."

Caleb looked at her; he couldn't contain his humor. He laughed as she looked at him dumbfoundedly. The relationship vibe was definitely there. Caleb was just Caleb in her eyes, and he could just be himself, with no one to impress and no expectations required of him. Kacey was taking the lead and giving him something he could feel. Unbeknownst to Caleb, Kacey had started to compete with a woman he knew had his heart. His time spent with Bethany began to decrease tremendously.

They walked to the restaurant that Kacey wanted to experience. She insisted on paying not because of the cost but to show her gratitude for his friendship and the support he provided in helping her reconnect with her faith. Caleb finally relented after her persistent requests. Although he felt a bit awkward about it, he sincerely appreciated her gesture, and Caleb recognized the positive influence he had on her life.

Dinner was fun and light-hearted as their conversations over the phone were enhanced with them looking at each other and being able to enjoy the mental banter with emotions and gestures only felt or heard in voice inflection over the phone. To their surprise, they had an open and honest conversation about sex. Kacey made known her husband was her first. Caleb looked at her.

"Really?"

"Yes, really. I didn't want to have a lot of different experiences. Don't get me wrong, I found myself in a few situations that almost lost that card of only one...being young, fun playing around, and the chemistry getting the best of me. But when it came to that…somehow, I sobered up quickly. I wanted to know who the father of my children was."

Caleb listened as he thought of Tonya in a healthy way, hearing Kacey talk. Caleb, being curious, had to ask, with a slight smile on his face… "Sooo, since your divorce…?" He inquired without asking the remaining part of the question.

Kacey smiled… "Oh, you are trying to get some?"

Caleb bit back, grinning broadly, "You, offering." He stated with a slight turn of his head as he looked at her before, letting the humor overtake them. They both laughed as they were happy just talking. Kacey wasn't ready, and neither was Caleb. But the idea was… if and when will we…? The restaurant had become quiet as it was winding down to close when the waiter asked if they wanted coffee and dessert. Caleb stated yes, and it was going to be his treat. Kacey bowed her head graciously.

As the conversation continued, no one in earshot… Kacey asked the inevitable.

"So, what about you, Caleb. I know you are not carrying around a celibacy card."

Caleb was happy he caught himself before taking a sip of the coffee placed in front of him just moments ago…. He thought about her direct bluntness. Kacey held up her cup of coffee with a look of *What you see is what you get. You know I will speak my mind. Don't let this visit fool you…*

Caleb shook his head and just looked at her. "You ask the hard questions, Kacey."

"Oh, you're the one to talk with the questionnaire over the phone."

Caleb answered with one word. "Truth."

"Yeah... so...?"

Caleb wanted to be completely open. He felt comfortable in doing so... Kacey had given so much about herself regarding her divorce and marriage throughout their conversations prior to her visit. He knew she was lighthearted about her question, but his mind was not.

"To be honest, Kacey, I carried the card until college. Straight out of high school with parents who knew what I did without me ever telling them. I didn't have a choice for privacy's sake."

Kacey smiled... "So, just for your privacy, you did nothing."

"YEAH, something like that. If you knew my mom or had ever met her, God rest her soul, you'd understand."

Kacey knew his mom was a painful subject and just nodded as he continued to talk.

"So, college became interesting, and I had my first child, as you know, while living in Africa. Only to marry my ex-wife Tonya... I was trying to live right at that time; however, after my divorce and my mother passing away. I can only say I was not pleased with my actions. I was a one-night stand kind of guy during that period of my life."

Kacey listened. Not saying anything, just listening as the conversation went on to the pain of divorce, the loss of a parent, and coping with life. As they walked back to his apartment. Kacey reached for Caleb's hand. He looked at her... She held it up and said. I feel you. They looked at each other, and Caleb felt her reassurance as they walked hand in hand, feeling at peace.

They made it back to his place, and he asked if she wanted

a glass of wine, as neither of them was ready for the night to end. Kacey made herself comfortable on his sofa as he brought her glass of chardonnay to her. They sipped in quiet each in their own thoughts. Kacey looked at Caleb, really looked at him, and realized she was truly attracted to him. The more she learned about him, the more appealing he became. Her mental plane of thought gauged her chemistry, and Caleb's personality and demeanor were pushing her chemistry and libido to an all-time high.

"Kacey, Kacey..."

Caleb called her twice as she stared blankly at him. He wondered where her mind went to be so intense and quiet.

"Kacey."

Her eyes refocused and looked at him. She caught herself before speaking her mind.

"You okay," Caleb asked.

"Yes. I'm fine. Sorry about that."

"Oh No, what were you thinking?"

Kacey didn't want to say. And deflected his questions.

"More about you. I was thinking. How has life been with you since your one-night stand?"

Kacey was pushing his buttons. Caleb mentioned his last relationship, naming Bethany. Since then, sex has been relatively easy to deny when he thought of her.

Kacey looked at Caleb. "So, you still... friends with benefits."

"It was for a while. But then she started dating others, and we just keep in touch. She is honestly a good friend."

Kacey knew then that Bethany was her opt. Kacey took a sip of her wine and asked no more questions. But Caleb did...

"So, you dodge the question earlier. How about you. Did you take up the celibacy card again after the divorce?"

Kacey smiled knowingly. "No. I did not. Being older and wiser and a divorcee... If the mood was right and the relationship was on point, I would be open. But I can count on one hand how many that has been. While I don't have the card, I still hold to my personal values."

Caleb nodded. Kacey's phone rang. She looked at the time. "Oh no, I forgot to tell my girls I made it here safe. Excuse me, Caleb, while I take this call."

Caleb gestured for her room. Watching her body sway as she walked away. He was indeed a man... He thought of Bethany... as he listened to Kacey's voice.

"Hey Lidya, Momma, sorry. I know, right. Yes, it is going well..."

Caleb drowned the rest of his wine. Put the glasses in the sink and thought....Kacey was so easy to be with, but his mind was clearly on Bethany.

Kacey thought about the woman named Bethany as she placed her travel bags across the threshold after getting back home to Atlanta, and then she dismissed Bethany. Kacey knew one thing about life. What you put your interest in was either going to grow into something or go away. If this was meant to be, it would be. She just had to continue to be herself, and she liked what was slowly developing with Caleb.

Their conversations and connections were not hot and

fast but slow and steady. The kind of relationship that had the potential to last. They put all their thoughts on the table. Maybe not in detail. But enough to know there was more to be learned- more to be addressed. Whether with each other or within themselves. Something she lacked in her first marriage with the age gap and coming to her own as a woman. She was enjoying the conversation and company of a man closer to her age, who saw her for her and not what he wanted her to be. Not an ideal thought of .... something he craved to have.

Kacey felt distant from Caleb at times. But her world, in regards to a relationship, was not the end product of marriage being the prize. After being there and doing that, she wanted substance and a lasting connection with someone to enjoy life with. Caleb was on point with her, and with the non-couple status, she knew where she stood with him and gave him the space to just be, which is what Caleb needed.

Time would tell all, Kacey thought as she told Caleb she would be away visiting her daughters at Martha's Vineyard. Caleb looked at her as she sprouted out information to him during a now routine Facetime call.

"I get absentminded around my babies, Caleb. I enjoy being a mother. Everything becomes secondary when I am with them."

She smiled as her eyes took on a far-away thought. "Phone calls don't get answered. I remember one time my job called, and the department missed a huge deadline. Oh my," Kacey rolled her eyes, emphasizing the upset. "My daughters said, Mom, you got a life; we love you... But that's not right. So, it's become a routine to give important people my eldest daughter's number. You never know what can happen in this life. So, if you find you want to call but can't reach me, please don't hesitate to call. I will return your call."

Caleb listened and took it all in, and his thoughts reverted back to Tonya, Bethany, and his mother. He listened to Kacey, as his heart said time would tell everything, but his spirit man gave him a moment. Caleb's inner being paused to relish the thought of accountability, transparency, and the small action of placing a priority on him outside the tangibles of life. He was thought of- and in that, he felt her respect for his time, the value of their interactions, and how important it is to stay connected. Relationship or no relationship.

She was not asking anything of him but to be himself. He was looking at her with a different set of eyes. And began to realize how much he was depending upon her. After hearing that, he could call her when he felt like it. His mind exhaled as he didn't know he was feeling some kind of way, knowing she was going to be away from his usual access. For the first time in a long time, he thought of Bethany and what she was up to... not as he missed her but in comparison to the woman he was enjoying, her voice of just meaningful and full of thought and care.

Caleb realized his communication and thoughts of Bethany had become few and far between. The call ended, and Caleb smiled and unconsciously dismissed Bethany and thought how much Kacey would enjoy her time with her daughters. He got a call from his son and daughters, and peaceful sleep and rest found him that night without the prayer room. All was well in his world.

As if on cue, Bethany reached out the next day, which Caleb discussed with Reese, who gave him an earful about it all.

"That demon is busy, Caleb."

"Stop calling her a demon, Reese. Bethany isn't a bad person."

Reese looked at him as if he had grown a third eye. "I wasn't implying that she was. But the spirit world is dual, Caleb. You, of all people, Mr. Minister, should acknowledge and know this."

Caleb didn't answer, nor did he look at Reese.

"See, you don't even want to acknowledge the truth." Shaking his head. "One day, it will become clear Caleb. Pray the hard prayer and truly let GO. Or are you still thinking she is the one?"

Caleb said nothing. Reese, knowing his friend, dropped the subject and made a comment on the game in front of them at the sports bar.

Caleb thought about Reese's question when he got home as his phone buzzed. Feeling a little happy thinking it was Kacey, only to see Bethany's number, he considered his inner feelings about it... as he answered her call out of habit.

As Bethany often did, she invited Caleb to watch a movie

after a long, stressful week of teaching. Bethany was known for cutting him off if she was interested in someone. Still, Caleb made himself available no matter the situation. So, he accepted her invitation.

Bethany sat between his legs, and he massaged her shoulders.

"So, how is everything going with Kacey?"

"It's good."

"So, are y'all officially together?"

"Nah, we haven't given each other titles yet."

"Why not? Don't you like her?"

"Yeah, but I am not in a hurry."

"Oh really! I know you like her."

"How do you know that?"

"We don't hang out as much anymore."

"That's not on me!" Caleb shouted. "You aren't interested in me anyway… not really… so don't put that on me, Bethany."

Bethany turned to face him, smiling to lower his tension; she wrapped her legs around his waist. Looking directly into his eyes, Bethany disarmed him by gently whispering kiss me, and he did. That night, the kiss was magical, and so was the connection that was made.

Caleb's loins ached as he thought of his interactions with Bethany physically. Bethany's easygoing ways kept his issues at bay. She was his fix, unbeknownst to him. As time took its course with his continued interaction with Kacey, Bethany was beginning to change. Caleb began to see her desire for him, but he knew he was just her fall guy, the backup plan. At least, that is how he pictured it. Caleb, sometimes perturbed, found himself answering Bethany's calls with the many excursions he and Kacey took as friends. He never told Bethany how much Kacey was beginning to mean to him, only that he would leave Kacey for her. He did this when Bethany had a moment of clarity, making her thoughts known that she truly wanted him. But Caleb didn't trust her sincerity in those moments due to past actions.

Caleb didn't want to acknowledge the peace of mind that Kacey was giving to his emotional well-being. Caleb walked into his room. Glancing at a picture of his mother, which he looked at many of times, stared back at him. He walked over, picked up the frame, and placed it back.

Later that night, for the first time since her return to glory, his Mom visited him in his sleep. She just stared at him, saying nothing for a while, then she smirked at him, and it broadened into a smile. Looking dead into his eyes as if reaching into his soul...she asked a question that hit him to the core.

IS GOD PLEASED with you?

Caleb was jolted awake from his sleep. He knew he was being lukewarm. That essence of man that God would sprue out of his mouth. He heard his mother say, "Leave her alone..." just as clear as day.

He looked around his room and thought of Elisha...Caleb knew he was being disobedient. He knew the right thing to do...Caleb took inventory of his life. Just as he was about to drift back to sleep, his phone buzzed. Looking at the clock, it stated it was 3 a.m. He sat up, fear washed over him, and his mind instantly went to Kacey.

Walking over to pick up his phone, he questioned how he felt. Questioning himself, speaking her name, "Kacey?" The overwhelming feeling of being a protector and the idea of her being in trouble. Caleb thought of Bethany, too, as he picked up the phone and read the text. He frowned at the message. THEN he laughed out loud as another text was followed by a different person with a different message. GOD TRULY had a sense of humor. He stood reading the texts twice from the two women in his life.

Caleb knew he was at a crossroads. He knew what he wanted... and wouldn't be denied. Would his flesh win or the spirit of God? Would he continue in this loop of loving Bethany or needing what was before him...Kacey. Time would tell all.

A YEAR LATER

Love Rewritten

I I

PRAYERS PRAYED

Caleb couldn't help but think about his new marriage as he listened to a guy from his small group talk about his recent divorce. Caleb, now in another marriage for almost a year, thought about his wife. Caleb kept a poker face as he replayed his own inner thoughts. The small group leader's words provided a revelation and confirmation about Caleb's personal thoughts and connection with his present wife.

Not saying much at all at the small group meeting, Caleb pondered all that was spoken. He knew he loved her. She was a wonderful woman and helpmate. They were living the dream and enjoying many of the world's amenities. She was very patient with him and proven to be loyal and faithful during Caleb's transition with his health and finances. But there was one problem....Caleb thought....How did I get here?

Caleb thought back... to his life after Tonya, and the woman that led to his new life God ordained, and now with his new wife... Looking back, Caleb was grateful for Grace and Mercy. His prayer room, on many occasions, became his bedroom, and he would spend many nights praying for forgiveness with his flesh.

He laughed at himself sometimes and thought about the Men's Retreat. Remembering the Scripture, God placed upon his heart judge not... for he who is without sin cast the first stone... He understood now more than he wanted to realize the temptation of the flesh with the Be Fruitful and Multiply desires blazing within himself.

He knew marriage would help with the fight. But an ordinary love just won't do, resonated within him. He knew love would not be enough. His next relationship had to be more than that. However, he found himself weak ...and his mother's words came at him in full force when he thought of his actions, which bombarded him.

Caleb heard the best way to get over someone was to find someone new, but his inner thoughts held him at bay from truly committing. During this period of his life, he thanked God for His love for him. Especially in regards to his life choices.

Caleb thought of his many escapades with his recycled love and how God was setting him up... making him see himself in ways he didn't want to see. He smiled as a scripture settled in his spirit.

Jeremiah 29:11-

For I know the thoughts that I think toward you,
saith the Lord, thoughts of peace, and not of evil, to
give you an expected end.

Caleb let his mind wander as the meeting was coming to a close. He wasn't open to sharing, nor could he share his illicit thoughts. Caleb lustfully fantasized about being physically and spiritually one with his wife and relentlessly ravishing Bethany. He knew he was wrong, thinking of Bethany as he knew it was adultery, but it fed him. Then Caleb thought back to his first decision... to take the leap and live the life he was now experiencing ...

The night of the mysterious text.

Caleb remembered the night when his mother visited him in a dream. His mind pondered over the voice that called to him and the individual text from the women who were in his life at the time. Being at the crossroads and with God truly working in him spiritually, he knew he had to make a decision. Would he continue to lean into his own understanding...or press toward the mark for the prize of the high calling of God...Remembering the text, it was the catalyst for taking a leap and committing to just one.

He saw the first text:

Why can't a man be a man? I mean, really, is it too much to ask for a bit of time and affection, or how about commitment...?

The text continued- but for some reason, Caleb wasn't interested in reading the rest as it reminded him of Tonya. The word *used* resonated within him, and considering the person behind the text, it had been weeks since their last meeting, which he didn't want to think about. Just as he was about to put the phone down, his heart skipped a beat with anticipation and fear, like he felt when he first got up to check the phone. As he was placing the phone down, it vibrated in his hand. This time, he wondered, and yet he knew who it was...

Caleb, I just woke up, and this was placed upon my heart -I don't know why... I pray all is well. Isaiah 11:2 *And the spirit of the Lord shall rest upon him, the spirit of wisdom and understanding, the spirit of counsel and might, the spirit of knowledge and of the fear of the Lord...*

Rereading the last text, a feeling of peace overshadowed him, and he didn't answer Bethany. For the first time, he did not jump when she called him, and his mind did not give her first priority. He thought about his dream, and another scripture came to mind from Amos 3:3 *Can two walk together, except they be agreed?*

Bethany wanted a life he couldn't give, and he allowed his flesh to get the best of him. But on this night.... His inner spirit that sought after God- Caleb allowed it to guide him and gave it free reign. He looked at Kacey through the eyes of God's Holy Spirit within him.

He answered her text: *I needed that.*
To which Kacey replied: *To God be the glory.*

Caleb met up with his father a few days later. He hadn't been doing too well since his mother's death. But Mr. Mitchell, understanding that God was in control, just missed his wife. However, he was internally grateful for his life and loved when his son stopped by to visit him. Mr. Mitchell, being spiritually observant, noticed that for the past few weeks, Caleb seemed like a different man. He questioned if Bethany had anything to do with it, as he hadn't heard Caleb talk of anyone else.

Caleb walked into his home house to see his dad watching a Saturday game with a bottle of apple juice.

"Hey, Dad."

Mr. Mitchell looked around, somewhat surprised but happy to see his son.

"Hey Caleb, I didn't hear you come in." Caleb reached down and hugged his father as a greeting, motioning for Mr. Mitchell not to get up. Caleb went to the kitchen, got a bottle of water, and then sat in the adjacent reclining chair and looked at the screen. They sat in silence for a while, just enjoying each other's presence.

"I see you watching the UGA game," Caleb stated.

"Yeah, it's okay. I'm looking forward to the game with Alabama and Auburn. You coming through?"

Caleb smiled as he knew his father too well. "Well, that is why I stopped by. I was wondering if you would like more than just my company that day?"

Mr. Mitchell took a sip of his juice as he considered what his son was indicating.

"You mean like Bethany? I haven't seen nor heard of her since your mother passed away, and I remembered your mother's thoughts about the young lady."

Caleb smiled, which caught his father off guard for the first time since his mother returned to glory. Mr. Mitchell studied his son, looking at him intently, and stated... "You different, Caleb."

"I am Dad, and so is the person I want you to meet."

Mr. Mitchell looked at his almost empty bottle of juice. "Hmph. You sound rather serious about this."

"I am Dad, and unlike the last two times, I am going to go about this the right way. Mom knew more than I wanted to give her credit. I need a righteous eye this time around. I want companionship as God ordained for Adam, as you found with Mom. I can't say I understood you with Mom. But... well, you know."

Mr. Mitchell understood Caleb and respected his son's concerns for him when he spoke of his mother.

"Caleb, I loved your mother, and yes, I do hurt knowing that she is not here with me. More than I would like to admit. But you speak your mind now here. We have always been that way, and I don't want it to change. It is what makes our relationship as father and son so endearing. Your mother knew this as well." Caleb nodded.

"So, is it a go, Dad?"

Mr. Mitchell looked around his home. He was a neat man, and he had a cleaning crew come by twice a week and an organizing crew once a month to help keep him on point with the pile-up of unnecessary things. But he stated his thoughts anyway. "If you won't be ashamed of the house."

Caleb laughed. "Dad, as clean as this house is, I could probably eat off the floor."

Mr. Mitchell laughed. "I don't advise you do that, though, Caleb. My shoes have been places." And they both laughed.

Caleb made his thoughts known to Kacey that he wanted her company and for her to meet someone important. Kacey, having the weekend free and open, traveled to meet Caleb. He invited her to his place immediately.

Kacey usually got a room at a hotel nearby; however, she enjoyed spending time with him, but since they were not in an exclusive relationship, she kept to her personal standards of living. She took nothing for granted nor assumed, including his space. Caleb appreciated her respect for his space, but he made it clear it was on him this time and for her to meet him at his place as they would be leaving immediately upon her arrival.

Kacey wondered what was up but asked no questions. She was just happy to be in his presence and his request for her time, which was happening more as of late. Caleb met Kacey at the entrance of his apartment. Placing her luggage next to his sofa.

"Are you good Kacey? You ready to go?"

Kacey laughed. "You haven't told me where. I'm comfortable in traveling clothes."

In Caleb's eyes, jeans and a white shirt accentuated her chest but was long enough to cover all her goodies; Kacey was classy in his eyes as she was dressed appropriately. He walked over to her and said let's go. She laughed as they walked to the parking deck and got into his vehicle, which was parked next to hers.

Mr. Mitchell looked out the window. Waiting and curious as to who Caleb was bringing home. As Caleb's car drove up, he looked at the passenger seat and discerned her. She was a breath of fresh air just upon her look, and as she got out of the car, she looked very down to earth.

She smiled and looked at Caleb curiously. "Where have you brought me, Caleb?"

Caleb looked at her... "To one of the most influential people in my life, next to God. I want you to meet my father. As you know, my mother has passed away, and no other woman has stepped foot in this house since she passed."

Kacey looked at Caleb, understanding what was about to take place. She felt honored and overwhelmed. Caleb as though he read her mind. "Kacey, you look fabulous. Don't fret."

She smiled at his reassurance as an older and still handsome version of Caleb stepped from the door onto the porch to greet her. He looked at her, and she felt as if he could look into her soul, and she felt comforted by his presence. Mr. Mitchell thought...his wife would have approved, and he looked at Caleb. "Well, you two, come on in and make your-self at home."

Caleb sighed a sigh of relief, as did Kacey, and they both smiled as they held hands, knowing this was just the beginning, day one of their relationship beyond casual dating.

Kacey texted her daughters, informing them of her safe arrival as she waited for Caleb and his father to bring the refreshments from the kitchen. She couldn't think of a better way to get to know each other than over a game they all wanted to see. Her daughters were so happy to know all was going well with her.

Kacey and Mr. Mitchell enjoyed talking stats, football plays, and interacting. As the evening winded down, he talked about his wife and their years of marriage. Kacey looked at the pictures and noted Ms. Mitchell was a force to be reckoned with. Mr. Mitchell agreed and gave some ideas. Kacey paused at one serious story, which Mr. Mitchell told purposely to gauge Kacey's reaction.

Kacey heard the story and raised her hand, "I'm sorry, Mr. Mitchell. I know how serious that story is, but your wife has me thinking about my great-grandmother. That woman was feisty, and lord help you, she knew things that no one under-stood how." She turned to Caleb, "Your mother and I would have got along just fine; I would see my great-grandmother in getting to know her." She turned to Mr. Mitchell, "Thank you for sharing your life with me. I count it an honor."

Mr. Mitchell looked at Caleb and saw his son's thoughts toward the woman. He wondered if Caleb knew what he had brought home. Watching them both, Mr. Mitchell felt the strains of life pulling on him to go truly home. Seeing Kacey and talking with her, Mr. Mitchell hoped Caleb would do right so he could follow his love to glory.

Caleb and Kacey left his home, and Mr. Mitchell went into his prayer closet and thanked God for his prayers being answered. He talked to his wife's picture and felt a peace overshadow him. He knew she was also pleased. He left the room and turned in for the night, smiling as he was looking forward to Kacey's return visit, as she promised to cook them all a Sunday dinner. Since his wife's death, his home seemed like it breathed with life and was anticipating tomorrow.

The Relationship

Kacey was tired on the way back to his place. But she smiled at Caleb with slightly closed eyes. She sighed, and he looked over at her. "I really like your dad, Caleb. Thank you for allowing me to meet him. I consider it an honor," she said breathlessly.

Kacey didn't take for granted the idea of them being in a relationship. She didn't want to assume. So, she steered clear of the subject until Caleb made the first gesture or comment to solidify the importance of the day. Caleb smiled, not saying anything. He kept his eyes on the road, and his hand crossed the mid-console of his SUV, grabbed her hand, and squeezed it. He said nothing as he parked the vehicle and led her to his apartment door. Punching in his code. Kacey leaned against the door. Thinking about the day and all that occurred, she wanted to hear him speak the words she didn't want to assume. They walked in.

"Caleb, I..." Kacey started to speak. But Caleb didn't give

her a chance to finish her thought as the door closed, and he grabbed her around the waist and looked down at her. "I want you beyond a one-night stand, Kacey. I want you here beyond the friendship we have cultivated. I want you for all that you have been and are to me. I can't see life without you. You have become a beacon of peace, a place of solace in the most turbulent times. God knows my needs, and you are definitely beautiful inside and out."

He pulled her closer to him, and she felt his desire for her. Kacey looked at him, speaking her mind respectfully. "Say it, Caleb. Say it plain. I don't believe in assuming. Not with this... what are your intentions?"

Caleb leaned in to kiss her, and Kacey pulled back to keep him from completing the action. She continued, "I care for you too much as a person to play with your... no, really both of our inner peace of mind. Where is this going, Caleb? As friends, we are good where we are. Nothing beyond what you wish to give. But I can't move forward physically with you if we are not working toward marriage. I'm sorry... I just care too much to ruin this... as we are."

Caleb smiled as he repositioned himself and Kacey into a more intimate embrace. Quieting her final thoughts..."I totally agree, for it is written he who findeth a wife findeth a good thing, Kacey."

Kacey smiled. "Have you finalized your seeking?"

Caleb burst out laughing. "You truly know how to keep a man waiting with the questions."

Kacey laughed. Dropping her head, Caleb's hand reached up to catch her chin in order to place a kiss on her forehead. Titling her head upward, he looked into her eyes. And spoke the words she needed to hear. "I love you, Kacey, for just being Kacey. Yes, I am moving forward toward something more than just friendship."

He pulled her to him as she lay her head against his chest and heard his heartbeat. Caleb embraced her, cherishing her as her arms encircled around him. He placed his head on top of hers. Realizing they were a perfect fit. His desire for her grew. But... his mind wandered for a moment, and he dismissed it.

She looked up at him with a mischievous, playful look. "Is that really all of you..." She sashayed her body against his arousal as she finished her statement... "or is there more for me to know?"

Caleb busted out laughing. "Woman, you a mess."

Kacey looked up at him, feigning innocence with an inquiring look. "Hey, this woman has got to know. Are you an anaconda or just nicely endowed?"

Caleb pulled her to him again, looking down at her. "You want to find out?"

She shook her head, "No... Not tonight. This woman is going to sleep. One thing at a time. Today, I was invited into a very serious relationship. You don't give up all the cookies at one time. At least not before I cook your dad dinner..."

He laughed even more at her. "Can a brother get a kiss then? I want to lay claim you mine."

Kacey laughed. "Nope," and she meant it as she walked away, "but if you wait right here, I will be right back." She took her luggage into the guest room, which sealed her intentions for the night, only to return shortly with a book in hand.

Caleb looked at the book, and he smiled. He knew life was

going to be engaging with her. He watched her as she walked towards him, sitting on the sofa. Caleb got up and met her. He took her hand and led her down another hall toward the most sacred place in his apartment. They went in together to place all things in their proper place spiritually before physically. Caleb allowed her to enter his sacred space.

Kacey knew he was serious as he began to pray for their life and their individual walk with GOD. Feeling the presence of God, the fleshly desire denied, they retired for the night, each to their own space. They were happy with the new life they were about to embark upon.

Caleb lay in his bed hearing the sounds of his apartment, and his dreams took him to Bethany, the mocha brown Bethany. He jolted awake as his dreams had him sexually intimate with a woman, not his to take with his current situation. Caleb knew Bethany was a good person, but not good for him. In his weakest moments... he found himself seeking Bethany. As his mother stated, he disrupted her life. However, in Reese's mind, Bethany was the devil's #1 play card for tempting Caleb.

Caleb knew it was his stronghold- a temptation beyond doing the right thing, considering how he allowed his life with Kacey to be intertwined with Bethany. Reese wondered how long it would last, and he silently prayed for his friend. However, Caleb let his flesh get the best of him time and time again.

Kacey knew he was dreaming when she heard his moans in the other room, and Bethany's name was called from his lips. She knew his love for Bethany ran deep in his veins, but she still wanted him, Caleb, flaws and all. God help me, Kacey prayed. Questioning, was Caleb really ready to embrace all she had to offer?

Mr. Mitchell stuffed himself, and so did Caleb. Both were just outdone by Kacey's cooking skills. They all sat in the den after washing the dishes. Kacey sat next to Caleb as he insisted. Mr. Mitchell beamed ear to ear over the whole idea as they sat and discussed one topic after another until Caleb saw his father getting tired. It was getting close to 8 pm.

The evening came to an end, and Kacey promised to visit real soon. Mr. Mitchell making her promise. She smiled as she and Caleb walked to the vehicle, and Mr. Mitchell went back inside, shutting off the lights within the house for the evening. Caleb held her hand during the ride back to his place, a very happy man. Kacey made it back to Atlanta, and he eventually called Bethany and fell from grace unbeknownst to Kacey.

Caleb's phone rang.

Reese, not for wasting time when telling Caleb about himself, started in on him without a hello...

"Caleb, I heard about Bethany..."

Caleb looked at the phone silently, with a bit of fear and annoyance due to Reese's statement.

Reese, not outdone, let the silence sit for a moment with the call... "See, Caleb, this is why I say she is your demon."

Caleb said nothing. As he knew the turmoil he created with Bethany, he would have to atone for it. God help him.

"Hello, Caleb; you still there?" Reese stated, ending the filled empty silence with the question.

"Let me be Reese. I know I have issues..." Caleb finally stated.

Reese, not wanting to be too hard but being truthful, did not let up. "We all have a cross to bear and a sin to overcome, Caleb. But man, sheesh, it's how we deal with it and how we ask God for guidance, Caleb. Don't think you are the only one in this world with issues." Reese heard Caleb sigh.

"I know Reese. But this girl here. I mean, it is like an addiction with Bethany."

"Sooo, you are owning up to your lower member having problems?"

Caleb chuckled a little. "Well, *the Be fruitful and multiply* is definitely wanting and urging with Bethany. That is for sure. I don't know about having an issue with my member, but when it comes to Bethany. That is a firm, and I do mean firm affirmative."

"Caleb, man, you got to do better. You got a good woman and you still chasing?"

"I know, but I don't want to hear it, Reese."

Reese knew when he had pushed the buttons, eased off Caleb, and talked politics and other aspects that were amusing to the world. They both laughed and sent up a heaven help us before they ended the call. But Reese's words of wisdom were lost on Caleb as he continued living in his flesh.

Months later

Caleb looked at his phone as he traveled on 285 to meet Kacey. Wanting to hear from Bethany before he reached his destination to spend the weekend with Kacey, he called out his car phone system.

"Call Bethany." His car phone dialed and clicked over only to hear. *You have reached the voice mailbox of...*

Caleb disconnected the call. After his months messing around with Bethany, knowing he was in a committed relationship, he knew this was not the time to be bothering her. But Reese was not lying, and being truthful he wanted to bury himself within the warm contours of Bethany.

It was like revenge for Caleb and an unquenchable lustful dessert. He loved the feel of her and the ideology of her that fed a part of himself that longed for her company, not to mention the arousing pleasure. Also, the profound hope of maybe just maybe she could be his....and he -her covering... But an inner voice nudged him, and he ignored it with a price. He was not being spiritual and was leaning unto his own thoughts indulgingly. After traveling a few miles, his phone rang.

"Hi, Caleb."

Caleb smiled, happy to hear the voice he wanted to hear.

"Hey, Beth."

"So, what has you calling? What's up."

Caleb felt her distance and wished it were the other way around. "Just checking in; its been a while."

"Yeah, it has."

"Anything else, Caleb?"

"Nope," he heard himself say.

"Okay, well, I got to go, me and the girls are out on the town. Have a good one, Caleb."

"Oh, and Caleb,"

"Yeah?" He asked quietly, feeling her distance.

"I will call you soon. I have great news to share. Will you be around later this week?"

Caleb heard hope and cheered up. "Yes. I look forward to your call."

"Cool, talk to you later. Bye."

"Bye."

The call disconnected.

Three days later

Caleb received a call from Bethany and rushed over to her place when she asked if he was free. He listened to her discuss her book that was about to be published. It was refreshing to hear her passion for the book instead of her usual bouts with previous men she had dated or been out with recently.

"Can you believe it, Caleb, me an author?"

Caleb listened and smiled at her success and thought about the countless days he spent hearing her read the manuscript to him. She was truly a great writer, and the stories she wrote were very insightful. He and Bethany talked until they could talk no more, and one thing led to another as they both felt the attraction of their chemistry. Caleb enjoyed the rest of the evening, repeatedly entering Bethany's cavernous warmth and sweetness, and in that one shared moment, Bethany's distant attitude waned away as they spent more time together. But not without the flaws of their fragile reunion.

After months of spending time together, Caleb was still not seeing Bethany's desire to be with him exclusively. So, he started distancing himself. Caleb knew Bethany was loving the past attention as she began to call him more. Caleb loved seeing her call during his time with Kacey. He would give Bethany only a curt response or say I'm busy. He was playing her and didn't care at the time. Caleb was enjoying life on his terms. He was finally getting the results he wanted to see from Bethany...She was finally resenting not having his time.

Bethany, being fed up with his actions, kept placing ultimatums to cut all ties with him, letting her thoughts be known. She laid all the cards on the table, letting him know she wanted more from him. She stressed it more, especially since he kept clearly stating he would leave Kacey. Bethany, in so many words, dropped the ball and strongly implied-*"then prove it"*. Caleb wanted to do neither and played on her emotions. He enjoyed the ritual of making up with Bethany in her moments of weakness for his pleasure.

In Caleb's mind, he knew what Bethany wanted. She wanted him to prove himself- like he did with his divorce. She wanted him to make his intentions clear despite himself, and he resented her for it. Caleb saw Bethany at times as needy and not sympathetic to his pain. He, at times, thought of her as a Tonya. As time took its course, Caleb enjoyed the physical, and Bethany felt the strain of their ups and downs, and she stopped calling.

Caleb, hating the feeling of being rejected, sealed her fate of truly not being for him, and at that moment, he felt free in his spirit. But he was troubled again, and he leaned not into his own understanding and, in his anguish, took the higher ground. He instinctively knew the best thing was for him to continue with Kacey. On Valentine's Day, he proposed and received his father's blessings.

Caleb enjoyed a lovely, quiet weekend with Kacey, and no Bethany in the picture. He wanted to take his relationship with Kacey to the next level. Yet Kacey kept the physical contact to a minimum. He knew she was open to giving it up, but for some reason, she was holding out.

Feeling the strain of the lack of physical intimacy, Caleb deepened a kiss with Kacey that led to heavy petting, letting her know he wanted more. Kacey thought about the ring on her finger and wanted to give in.... But her memory of hearing Caleb's moans and the name Bethany resonating from his room while he slept kept her at bay. She returned the kiss as she also wanted more but could not move past her thoughts. She broke away from Caleb and stated, "I'm not ready, Caleb." She looked up at him as he closed the windows to his soul and leaned his head upon hers. He heard the words he didn't want to hear.

"Plus, you know more than I-we are not ready for that." He wanted to question her thoughts as to why... but knowing his ways did not press the issue. They enjoyed the remainder of their time together. Sexually frustrated, he waved as Kacey's car drove down the parking deck to return to Atlanta.

As if on cue, he found himself thinking about Bethany, and he called her after not talking to her for months. Bethany answered and then gave him a piece of her mind about men and himself, and so did Reese when Caleb slipped up and mentioned Bethany during a call. But Caleb, being Caleb, dismissed their thoughts from his mind and continued to be as he wished. And after hearing Bethany's rant and ravings.

He bided his time and found himself at her place, playing between the sheets until the morning light.

Kacey, visiting Caleb on a Saturday afternoon to work on a few wedding arrangements, stopped by to talk to Mr. Mitchell on her own and told Caleb to meet her at his father's place. Walking in, Mr. Mitchell was happy to see Kacey and even more so without Caleb. She was becoming the daughter he never had, and he was delighted to finally enjoy this aspect of life that was denied by Caleb's ex-wife, Tonya.

Mr. Mitchell listened to Kacey talk about wedding arrangements. She paused as she looked at her soon-to-be father-in-law. "Mr. Mitchell, what is the one thing I need to know about Caleb? I am working on my wedding vows, and I want to be sure I have them right."

Mr. Mitchell heard her thoughts and was thankful to God for her insight. He patted the seat so Kacey could sit next to him. He commenced to discuss Caleb's life as a child with a mother who didn't establish an emotional connection with him due to her own life trials and tribulations.

"Caleb has tendencies, struggling with love and trust. Being patient and hearing God's voice in everything you do will be the key to him. Especially if you hope to endure this journey with my son for the long haul. I speak from experience. Caleb's heart is in the right place, but like his mother, he battles inner turmoil. I pray for the day he can overcome."

Mr. Mitchell patted her on the knee. Kacey leaned in and gave him a side hug. Grateful for the talk. She needed to hear

Mr. Mitchell's words. Kacey knew Caleb had internal turmoil along with one aspect of his life that kept him distant from her at times. But she kept it to herself and continued asking God for guidance.

Mr. Mitchell saw her inner spirit. He sent up a special prayer for her... knowing that she would need spiritual guidance and prayer. Mr. Mitchell remembered his first years of marriage and the voice of God giving him his divine purpose, the wisdom of understanding what prayer would do, and the unconditional love for Mrs. Mitchell. He questioned God about Kacey. *Will she be able to endure with my son as I did with my wife?* Mr. Mitchell loved his wife deeply in spite of...

He watched Kacey for a moment as Kacey took pen to paper, and a settled peace overshadowed him.... *It shall be with Kacey,* resonated within. He saw her strength to look beyond Caleb's faults and see the broken man who needed a virtuous woman beside him. But as the voice spoke to him. Mr. Mitchell knew that man had a choice. He remembered the many nights crying out to God through the pain. He remembered the hurt and the doubt that crept into his spirit. He knew it took a personal walk and a relationship with God. Caleb's father smiled.

Mr. Mitchell, using himself as an example, gave Kacey more insight into his son's life. He talked about his role as a father and a husband with all that his wife endured and what his selfishness brought on by wanting a child and that child being a male did to his wife. He also discussed with Kacey the suffering of Caleb and the redemption of God's grace in his son's life. Then Mr. Mitchell went inward with his thoughts. *I have to think about this: has God ordained Kacey, as I look back over everything that has endured and is still being endured with Caleb?* He looked at Kacey thoughtfully.

Kacey took it all in gaining a greater understanding of her soon-to-be husband. She knew God was on her side and that Caleb was an answer to her prayers. But she had work to do. Kacey hugged Mr. Mitchell. She truly enjoyed his wisdom and spiritual insight. Her daughters did, too. She found out they called him from college.

Mr. Mitchell was spoiled by all his grandchildren and the new relationships with Kacey's daughters, who doted on him. Kacey's daughters were beautiful and very well-mannered. Mr. Mitchell saw the love they had for others as it was given to them by their parents. He even talked to Kacey's ex one time as he wished Kacey a heartfelt congratulations for her upcoming marriage. Mr. Mitchell saw Kacey as a woman who knew her worth. Her strength of character was what Caleb needed.

He beamed as he watched his son enter the room. He couldn't be more happy or proud of his son. But he prayed for him. He knew Caleb still wrestled with his flesh. Although in the midst of it all, Mr. Mitchell finally felt at peace and a peace surrounding his son's life. He knew his temptations were still causing havoc, but with Kacey's strength and insight, he saw what others did not see, and he let go... Thanking God.

Caleb walked into the house to see his fiancé waiting on his father, fixing him a plate of food she had cooked. She walked into the kitchen to get Mr. Mitchell a cup of apple juice and smiled at her soon-to-be father-in-law with so much love and concern. Something he never saw with Tonya. Caleb didn't compare Kacey; it was just a beautiful observation.

His children loved Kacey as she came into town one weekend during their visit, and it was a beautiful time filled with love. He enjoyed speaking with her daughters. They were brilliant like their mother, and he found himself very protective of them. He saw them as an extension of himself, like his own daughters.

Caleb felt at peace as he walked Kacey into his still rented apartment after visiting his father and running errands for their upcoming wedding. Mike and Tonya even sent a cold congrats, a card given to the children to hand to him, which he found funny and a little disturbing. It appeared his mother's thoughts about Mike and Tonya were showing signs of her prophetic thoughts. He sent up a prayer. Life...it was finally beginning to make sense to him. He thought of his life with Tonya and how he felt looking at the cold congrats... He smiled- he was starting to embrace his new life with a little peace of mind.

12

MORE THAN IMAGINED

Caleb woke up to a knock on his apartment door from a state official; his father had passed on to glory. He braced himself, holding onto the door frame as the official gave an account from the cleaning personnel who found Mr. Mitchell peacefully lying on his back in bed, and from the looks of it, he had died in his sleep as no foul play was seen within the house nor with Mr. Mitchell. Caleb nodded, as he knew with the life his father lived, he expected him to go peacefully as he was in good health physically yet spiritually weak with life.

Caleb knew his mother was the love of his father's life, as well as himself. However, his father understood Caleb was the future. Caleb turned to see the woman behind him. She had become, in more ways, a pillar to lean on and a word of wisdom in time of need. Caleb thought of his father. The one person in the world who knew him, loved him and stood by him. But Kacey was showing her resilience; Caleb's spiritual insight forced itself within his anguish, leaving a Godly thought. *He knew you would not be alone...*

Thankfully, Kacey was visiting. She came out of the guest bedroom as Caleb closed the door. He told her of his father's passing, and they both cried and held each other in comfort. Caleb leaned on Kacey...

Caleb reminisced on the past few weeks. Grateful for Kacey's love and support after his father passed away was a blessing in the midst of sorrow. But he cursed Bethany for her actions toward him. Even in his time of need, she did not reach out, just like she had done with his mother. Caleb leaned into the embrace of Kacey more as she thought of his well-being above her own desires. He relished in her thoughts about the wedding. As his father was an intricate part of their relationship, Kacey felt it was best to postpone the wedding. They both felt they needed to grieve and give honor to Mr. Mitchell's life before starting a new one.

Caleb loved Kacey's sunderstanding. She became his lifeline and helper in the time of his grief. As love bears all, she was a foundation he could stand upon. Her undying love became his peace.

6 weeks later...

Caleb walked into his job and saw the pile of work that was waiting for him after taking all the time allotted to him for bereavement. He looked at the pile of papers and folders on his desk; he didn't have the energy to care. But when he began organizing files, his business line binged, and he thought, *Really, I just made it back, and they are already calling like this?* Caleb looked and noticed it was a text from Bethany.

Hey there sexy, why haven't you called.

He looked at the phone and shook his head. *No, not again,* he said to himself. His supervisor came in, and they discussed the next project that demanded his undivided attention. After talking with his supervisor, Caleb was elated to discover that his job finally had an opening at their Georgia office. But Caleb had to wait for the position personnel to finalize their work before he could assume the job. Considering the last text, he was happy about the updated information about his transfer, not to mention the benefits of a new business phone line that would cut all ties with Huntsville, Alabama, that specifically needed to be buried.

Three days later, around lunchtime, Reese called, letting him know he was in the area. They met around the corner a few blocks away from Caleb's job at a local diner in MidCity, Alabama. Reese looked at his friend, smiling proudly.

"You look better Caleb. And Kacey is the one, I like her. She cool people."

Caleb nodded, lost in thought.

Nothing got past Reese when it came to Caleb.

"Spill it, man."

"I got a text three days ago."

"Reese put his fork down. You got to be kidding me. Bethany?"

"The one and only," Caleb said, looking at Reese as he picked up a fry.

Reese shook his head, "She got a way with timing, man. You didn't answer, did you?"

"Heavens no. I don't have time for that. I love my fiancé." Caleb looked at Reese, "Kacey is all that you say and more. Especially after all I have been through. Bethany hasn't been there for me. She only thinks about herself. I need more than what she can offer."

Reese took a bite of steak, listening to his friend.

"She is still your demon, Caleb. I see her."

Caleb looked up. "I denounced that Reese. I can't keep looking back. I have to move forward."

Reese dropped his fork with a resounding clank. "Tell that to your member below. I know you, Caleb."

"Kacey is more than enough, Reese."

Reese raised his fork and knife. Pointing the knife edge at Caleb....

"REMEMBER YOU SAID THAT and BRAND It on your soul. I will keep you in prayer- that you remember Kacey is a GOD send. Bethany is not for you. That is my stance. But you..."

"No buts, Reese. Plus, I'm leaving Huntsville in a few months, like you. I will be COMPLETELY SETTLED in the Metro Atlanta area. Happy for it cause it puts me closer to my children as well. Not to mention, my daughter is thinking of going to college at one of the AU center schools."

Reese nodded. He was happy to hear his friend was leaving Alabama for a fresh start.

Caleb and Kacey looked at homes months ago before his father's death, and they settled on a spacious 3300-square-foot brownstone home. Kacey held firm on a home that would house the entire family of children should they visit. Yet cozy enough for them to enjoy alone. Caleb shook his head on the day of signing. He sat down as his name stood out on the paper as primary and Kacey as secondary. Either one of them could afford the home. But it was a joy as they sat together, happy to be starting a life together.

Kacey made it clear to the realtor that my future husband has the final say. Caleb felt so much pride in hearing those words as they discussed the final information to retain the keys. The realtor handed the keys to Caleb, and he gave them to Kacey. Now it's up to you to make it a home babe. Kacey beamed with pride. Yes, sir, Mr. Mitchell, and I am looking forward to you finally being with me in Atlanta. Caleb returned to Huntsville to finalize his preparations to move, but Bethany was silent in reaching out to him. Caleb missed her and resented her at the same time.

Kacey and Reese came into town and visited Caleb's home church in Alabama together. Caleb walked into the church with Kacey on his arm. He situated her on the front pew as he walked toward the pulpit with the rest of the ministers. Reese sat in the pew listening to Minister Mitchell and was thankful for his friend's leap of faith and upcoming new life in Metro Atlanta. However, it was only a matter of timing; Caleb's desire took root in fertile soil.

13

CALEB'S CROSS

Caleb was a kept man physically. While engaged to Kacey, he had his fun. Whoever said my man won't cheat. Don't understand the nature of how some men can be if they truly want to do so. Knowing marriage was his only thought toward the future. Yet Caleb abandoned his commitment when it came to Bethany. That sweet mocha brown Bethany.

He knew he was wrong. But he resented Bethany and put her in the place of Tonya. Caleb lashed out at Bethany with his actions, especially after months of trying to connect with her, only to have her dismiss his contact. He returned in kind when she finally tried to reach out to him. Eventually, time got the best of them, and they reconnected.

Caleb thought he had sealed Bethany's fate of truly not being there for him and cutting all ties until he received an email.

> *Dear Caleb, I hope this email finds you well. So sorry to hear about your father. Would you give me a call? I only need two minutes of your time. Please and thank you! You can reach me at 256-555-xxxx.*

Caleb reread the email. Outdone that, his inner world crashed, and his lustful desires hit him in full force. *Bethany.* Periodically, over time, he followed her social media page, and he was delighted at the success she posted and shared with the world. He was truly happy for her. However, after reading her email, he realized his actions of surfing her on the internet... aided in quelching his desire, and those moments fed his addiction. He didn't want to reach out as he was now in a relationship and had denied himself as he didn't want to connect via through social media. But he felt okay within his spirit to just look.

However, seeing her words in the email. He had barriers of restraint that flagged his actions as being seen or discovered. So, he responded immediately, as if time had been too long, and he was happy to hear from her, thinking about what harm could an email do? However, if Caleb knew in advance what his words meant to her. He would have kept his thoughts to himself.

Bethany responded, letting him know she was still thinking of him spiritually and life-wise as a candidate for her always and forever. He responded the only way he could, truthfully and without wisdom or tact.

Bethany, it's not by happenstance that you reach out; you've
been strongly on my mind lately. I came home from church
a couple of days ago, and I literally fell on my knees.
I told God to remove my thoughts of you or make way for us
to be together.

Once again, they found themselves reconnected with numerous calls and texts. Caleb created fake business meetings in Huntsville to help him transition into his new job in Atlanta. Although it was all a front in order to spend time with Bethany. Caleb not being sexually active with Kacey was taking its toll, even more so since they were living together. But Bethany was willing and ready.

Bethany knew he was with Kacey. This he did not keep from her. However, at times, it did put them on non-speaking terms. Caleb, knowing Bethany would wait it out by pleading and whining like any male would do to have his way. But it hurt Caleb to do so. He played the game with Bethany, but not as a *used female*, as he genuinely thought of her with love.

But pain loves misery, and Caleb, upon reconnecting with Bethany, wanted her. At the same time, he gained the benefits of a troubled mind. Torn between knowing what was right and feeling the hurt caused by his divorce, Caleb, in his mind, placed Bethany in the same category as Tonya. Bethany's repeated actions and patterns, presented over time, displayed a mentality that her convenience was more important than his pain. He became angry at the fact that when he needed her, she was not there. He resented her continued lack of respect. Her constant change of being with other men and not genuinely wanting him. He thought about it all as his body betrayed him time and time again.

He knew Bethany was feeling his indifference as he played with her emotions. Intentionally, he was tampering with fire when he answered calls when he shouldn't, telling Bethany his whereabouts and with who. He was hurting Bethany with his time spent with Kacey. Caleb was purposefully pulling Bethany along with no thought of commitment. He would have committed if he only believed Bethany was serious.

Caleb considered Bethany's action. It was as if Bethany blamed him for his divorce and for not being the man she wanted him to be. *But she never took the time to see me!* Caleb thought within himself. "Redial Bethany," he requested from the system, and the phone line repeated...*You have reached the voicemail box of....*and Caleb became angry and lashed out at Bethany all over again within his mind. *I'm through with her,* and he indulged himself with Kacey.

Caleb felt a different feeling of being rejected due to Bethany's actions of no call, no show, or concern. The feeling finally allowed him to move as he should have months ago. He finalized his move to Atlanta by making the last leap and cutting the ties of opportunity with Bethany. Caleb changed his private phone line and was thankful for his new address, living with Kacey. Spiritually, he was grateful as he mentally put parameters in place to physically complete his move to Atlanta, leaving Huntsville and his wayward habits behind.

I4

BETHANY'S LOSS CHANCE

Fertile Soil: 6 months later

Months went by, and Caleb didn't think about Bethany. But Bethany, like most times, found herself wanting Caleb in his absence... Bethany was upset and very happy at the same time. She missed her friend, and with inward self-reflection, she laid aside all her fears of playing it safe with Caleb. Bethany wanted more from Caleb, but Bethany couldn't overcome their starting point.

Once a cheater, always a cheater, she thought. But then discredited it against Caleb. He was upfront with her since his divorce. Bethany looked at the email from her publisher. She was elated and was experiencing the joy of the upcoming release of her new book. Bethany let her writing memories overtake her...which led to days when she read the manuscript to Caleb. Trying hard to distract herself, Bethany decided to leave her home and go to the bookstore to work on some of the final marketing ideas. However, thoughts of Caleb grew more intense, and she decided to answer the call of her heart and reach out to him. Looking at her phone directory for the last time, she spoke to him. She saw the missed calls from Caleb, and upon dialing the number, she received a computer-generated message.

The number you have reached is not in service; please check your number and dial again.

It was their way after a major upset- not *speaking* with each other for months on end. However, she was not going to let the past get the best of her, Bethany considered the non-communicative months, and she opted to send him an email.

Caleb sat at his home office desk, surfing social media and thinking of the unthinkable as an email populated. "Bethany?" His spiritual thought looked at the trash icon to delete, and a strong thought, *no no no...* overrode his spiritual gently nudge. *Plus,* he thought, *she's in Alabama, I'm in Georgia...how would words hurt?* He clicked her link.

Calmness soon swept over Bethany after reading Caleb's reply. He noted he had been following her on social media and was happy to share how proud he was of her success as a soon-to-be author. The words he wrote solidified her desire to confess her love and desire to be in a real relationship with him. She wanted more than a casual situation and desired marriage as her heart began to turn to him.

Caleb read her thoughts with mixed feelings as he faced the reality of his pending marriage. He looked around his office room and heard Kacey humming a tune from down the hall. His spirit felt the rise of past torments, and he dismissed the feeling. It was Bethany.

Once again, Bethany and Caleb found themselves re-connected with numerous calls, texts, and mini rendezvous during limited business meetings in Huntsville, Alabama, to spend time with each other. Bethany could not deny the fact that Caleb's move to Atlanta and close proximity to Kacey disturbed her. Bethany began to question him about the direction they were going.

On one particular visit to Huntsville, Caleb spent the night with Bethany. After a late dinner after a business meeting, with tears streaming down her face, Bethany explained to him that if he was not serious about committing to her, then they needed to end things now. Caleb kept himself in check. He knew he was treading a slippery slope. Caleb reassured Bethany of his love for her. He told her that he needed some time to figure things out, but he wasn't going to lose her again, even if that meant bringing her closer to him.

Within months of reconnecting, Bethany made plans to move to the Atlanta area. Caleb helped her land a new job, and she began to search for a place where they could start their new lives together. Finding both came easier than they anticipated; Bethany considered it as the confirmation she needed, giving affirmation that she was making the right move. For Caleb, it made his inevitable secret harder to hide, and Bethany's constant inquiries about Kacey did not make it easier.

Bethany knew their B&B trips only led to him going back to Kacey. But thoughts of his situation washed from her mind each time she found herself in his embrace. She believed that moving to Newnan would soon solidify all their plans, with conversations happening on a daily basis. However, her actions with moving seemed to do quite the opposite. Bethany began to ask Caleb about his timeline plans to move in with her. Caleb's frustration grew as he started to feel that she was pressuring him to leave the woman who had been there for him during some of the toughest times of his life. He convinced Bethany that she was trying to have things her way and in her timing. For once, Caleb wanted to be in control of his fear of being with Bethany.

However, Bethany had a renewed sense of hope as her plans to move to be with Caleb in metro Atlanta were in the works. With a new job secured and a god-sister who provided a place to lay her head just forty minutes from Caleb's residential location, she waited for their apartment to move in with Caleb.

Caleb, keeping his thoughts to himself, enjoyed his fall from grace, talking with Bethany and spending time with her. He even volunteered to help her move her stuff to Georgia. Being persuaded by their love, Bethany was sure that what the devil meant for evil, God had worked it out for their good. She thought back to the day at the grocery store, the walks in the park, the first kiss, and the day that they were naked and unashamed. Surely, this had to be God bringing them back together once and for all. Caleb, however, was not entirely convinced that her noncommittal ways were really gone, which showed after her move to Atlanta and a misunderstanding between them yet again.

Hidden Seeds Settling into Atlanta

The few previous relationships she had been in were taking their toll after Bethany settled into her Georgia life without Caleb. Still, it only made her miss Caleb all the more. But she soon realized that trusting him was like walking on sinking sand, and loving him would keep her in a drowning state. Bethany knew Caleb was seeing her in the midst of this Kacey, but Caleb had reassured her that he would break it off. Bethany considered Kacey like herself, just a close friend of Caleb, by the way he described their relationship. However, Bethany had reservations about Kacey's interactions with Caleb. This agitated Caleb, and Bethany once more felt his absence, only to receive calls from him to reconnect.

Bethany walked into the school, happy to be in the presence of her new job, and she thought of him. They reconnected by phone, and they both asked about their well-being. Which was typical for them. But Bethany still knew he was visiting her with Kacey, the other woman still in his life. She wondered how they were really doing with regard to each other.

Georgia proved to be fast-paced for Bethany, and with it came the opening of doors to her love life, not to mention her spirituality. The few previous relationships she had been in were taking their toll during yet another break from Caleb. Caleb was being the typical male with her emotions and she hated it. But the final straw hit her to the core... Bethany discovered the unthinkable...

Caleb became frustrated with Bethany's ongoing interrogations. He hated those moments when she made him think about how selfish Tonya was. Caleb listened to Bethany place her convenience over his own. He became angry at the fact that when he wanted her, she didn't want him. But when she called, he was supposed to jump to her beck and call. However, his libido, being physically wanton, Caleb complied more often than not.

Being empathetic to his situation, Bethany created her emotional distance. She reduced her contact with him as guilt made her accept his viewpoint as the truth.

Not being able to keep the lid of his boiling secret, Caleb revealed to Bethany why leaving Kacey wouldn't be so easy. He finally told her that he had proposed to Kacey several months ago, back on Valentine's Day.

Bethany thought, *how could he? Why did he play with my emotions and livelihood?* Caleb, coming to his bad-boy senses, realized he had opened Pandora's box, tried to soothe Bethany's thoughts, and assured her he wasn't really marrying Kacey. Struggling with this news, Bethany angrily refused to communicate with him. She did what was within her power to make a getaway from the cycle that continued to pierce her very soul.

Caleb, after numerous failed attempts to reach Bethany, sent an email. He lashed all his pent-up anger, telling Bethany without tact how he felt. Accusing her of not being supportive during the most difficult time of his life, noting his mother's death, and leaving him because of his financial issues. He released the withheld hurt steamed from his mother and Tonya upon Bethany. In his eyes, Bethany lost the edge of being different, and he resented it, considering his feelings for her.

Bethany thought about her interactions with Caleb. Her heart felt conflicted. But Bethany wanted to be free of him in every way that had depleted her mentally, spiritually, emotionally, financially, and physically. Caleb was tired of being used by Bethany and her non-committing ways. He thought of all the time he gave in to her demands with nothing for him to consider his own.

Yet with time, getting the best of them and their chemistry of attraction, Caleb and Bethany, still filled with hurt, eventually found themselves in each other's arms. Tears flowed down her face as Caleb lavished his desires, which were seen as affection to Bethany. He kissed her tears and trailed kisses down her neck to areas that made her scream in ecstasy as he tasted her.

To Caleb, it was his last goodbye. He gently stroked into her warmth, holding her in place, and whispered and sang sweet nothings into her ear. Lustfully, he drove into her repeatedly, thinking of his passionate experiences from times past, knowing this may be his last. The overwhelming desire and passion that Caleb was lavishing upon her, much to her surprise, won Bethany's trust as she could not imagine him leaving her. This was what made them one while they endured their ups and downs. It was their love for each other that she felt would override all obstacles. Her emotional connection was revived as Caleb called out her name with each stroke.

He increased his pace deeper and faster, carrying them into a wave of desire like never before. He freed all that he had within him, thrusting his pent-up lust into her, and she called out his name in ecstasy. Both lay spent, and Bethany confessed yet again her love for him. Caleb kissed her and started round two for the evening rendezvous, but this time, Bethany became a dessert as his tongue did all the talking.

Bethany questioned if Caleb would eventually leave Kacey like he divorced his wife, Tonya. But as Caleb showered and rinsed off the sweat from his body, his love thoughts waxed cold in regards to Bethany. He was finished chasing Bethany with an open door to leave Kacey. Caleb did the unthinkable in Bethany's eyes and got married.

Bethany soon discovered her lost chance as a blessing in disguise. Unknowing his action, yet feeling his distance, her heart grieved as her emotions, like a roller coaster, looped over in her mind of being heartbroken only to find healing again. The revolving aspects of dealing with Caleb repeated itself without shame; with highs and extreme lows, she just wanted peace.

After Caleb proposed to move forward with the wedding, Kacey questioned if it was the right time. She didn't voice it to Caleb she just nodded and went to her room and prayed. Caleb was happy about the turn of events with Kacey and went to visit his friend Reese to share the good news. Kacey, as she turned in for the night, thought of Mr. Mitchell and sent up a prayer. Opening her nightstand drawer, she looked at the sealed envelope. Her faith was renewed.

The next day...

Caleb reminisced on his life...as Kacey handed him the envelope. He looked at her and then the envelope. "It was given to me by your father. He wanted me to give this to you after our wedding. But I feel you might need to read it before...?" Caleb looked at Kacey, questioning if she knew. But dismissed the thought as he did not want to lose her with all that was going on in his life. She was his stability. Kacey patted him on the chest.

"I will leave you to read this alone. If you need me, you know where I am." Kacey smiled as she walked out of the den. He heard the sunroom's sliding glass door close. Caleb knew she went beyond the sunroom to the deck outside, and more than likely, a book and a cold beverage were waiting for her to pass the time. He smiled at how predictable she was, and he realized that he was content at that moment. He opened the envelope, and he heard his father's voice, reading between the lines. His dad knew he would transition to glory as he wrote the letter. Caleb's grief hit him anew as he read it. Past trauma and pain greeted him as well with his father's wished words of encouragement and spiritual insight. As Caleb read, he truly felt the absence of his father

Dear Son,

I am so proud of you and the woman you have married. I see so much of God in this... Be mindful to keep God first in all that you do, and this will be your saving Grace. For he who findeth a wife findeth a good thing. I am so looking forward to seeing your mother. I waited for you to find someone like Kacey and it makes my departure more peaceful. Find peace, my son. I will and have always loved you.

Dad.

The past tense of being married now in the present- was not lost upon Caleb, as the letter was written months before his father's death. Caleb cried as he reread the letter, feeling the loss of his parents. He knew this pain would not be forgotten, but he prayed for it to be easier to endure. Kacey found him and held Caleb as he cried out in anguish. Feeling the comfort of her touch soothed his inner spirit, and he knew marrying her was the right thing, even though his inner turmoil was eating him from the inside out.

Kacey, remembering the wisdom and thoughts of Mr. Mitchell, held on to dear life with Caleb. Some would call her weak. But she knew Caleb was a good man, just hurt, and considering how deep his pain went... he required a lot of patience and a lot of understanding. The measures she put in place were not known to others but clearly understood by Caleb. Time would be the final say to it all. Her faith in God transcended the thoughts and ideas of others and what her eyes and inner instinct gave her insight into.

The Wedding

Caleb, not seeing Bethany, was a happy man, especially after reading his father's letter. He found his balance once again, and by putting Bethany behind him, he enjoyed his fiancé and was now excited about his pending marriage.

The wedding was beautiful with Kacey's daughters and close family and friends. Caleb watched her as she walked down the aisle. He couldn't believe he was this lucky for a woman such as this... He knew his father was with him as he stood waiting for her to walk down the aisle. As she came into view. Caleb thought of all that he had endured, and tears swelled in his eyes. He couldn't believe he was this blessed, and he thanked God for his blessing. Kacey smiled, beaming proudly and clearly elated that who she was walking toward would be not only her husband but her confidant. She knew her life with him was a ministry. A walk of faith, with all that she knew of the man before her. But she thanked God for her new rekindled faith and the letter Mr. Mitchell gave to her personally. She would love Caleb for better or for worse. She saw his mother, and she saw his father. She found her place in the family. Caleb would have no need of spoil.

Being true to their beliefs as to when they wanted to consummate their relationship, Caleb was just happy knowing she was his and his alone... Even though his desire was heightened on their wedding day. The dream of her being his and his alone was now a reality.

They both reluctantly agreed to wait until after they made it to their honeymoon destination. But Kacey thought of spending the night at home after the wedding, before their flight the next day. Kacey had a change of mind as reality settled in...

Kacey walked up to Caleb and wrapped her arms around his waist, her cheek, feeling the contours of his back. He looked around and pulled her around to face him. Caleb leaned in and kissed her slowly. She returned the gesture with all the emotion she had after hearing all that he had endured from his father and with all the love she had to give with him finally being hers in the eyesight of GOD.

Caleb pulled away. "What's up, Kacey?"

She said nothing as she wanted him to feel, not hear her thoughts. She looked up at him.

"Kiss me, Caleb."

He smiled as his height kept her from just planting one on

him. He leaned in, and her hands reached around the back of his neck, which deepened the kiss.

Caleb held her around the waist, picked her up, and her feet dangled as they continued exploring each other intimately with the kiss. She wrapped her legs around his waist. Caleb pulled away from the kiss with a questioning look.

"Are you?"

Kacey smiled as she let one of her hands trail down his chest, enjoying his muscular build. She kissed him lightly and trailed kisses down the side of his neck to the opening of his chest. Then, she looked at him only to trace his full lips with the tip of her tongue.

Caleb groaned, all restraints for waiting going out the window as he held his wife with one arm around her waist and the other holding her bottom just a hand span away from where he wanted to bury himself in her warmth. He took long strides to their now soon-to-be shared master bedroom. His knee touched the bed, and she leaned back ever so slightly. Smiling with a look of desire and love that only she could give to Caleb.

"I love you, Caleb."

Caleb stopped and looked at her. Knowing she spoke a truth that he needed to hear and feel. She cherished him as he cherished her, a connection they made that transcended the action of becoming one physically. Their union was powerful as they connected mentally, emotionally, and ordained by God spiritually; they cried out, reaching their peak. Each spent they lay in each other arms for a while basking in the ambiance of their sealed union, now husband and wife....

Caleb looked at Kacey. Her hair was disheveled; she looked downright wanton and sexy. He kissed her lightly on the lips. She smiled and pulled him to her. "I want more of you." Caleb smiled...

Kacey looked at him. "I love the feel of you."

"My endowed or my anaconda?" Caleb teased.

Kacey looked up, smiling sheepishly; she teased back with, "You'll do."

"That's not what you said..." Caleb stated as Kacey placed her hand across his mouth.

"HUSH. You better not repeat what I said." Kacey laughed, embarrassed at his recant of her words in the throes of passion.

Caleb wrestled her hand from his mouth. As he mimicked her voice during their lovemaking... "I can't, I can't. Caleb... take I caca tayyyk."

Kacey jumped up. Straddling his waist. "Shhh Caleb... I didn't sound like that..."

Caleb laughed. "Yes, you did..." Kacey laughed at him as he wrestled her playfully, grabbing her by the waist and looking at her, in all her glory, waist up.

He wanted her and the idea of having her finally in his bed after watching her and yet not having her for years... His arousal grew.

He leaned forward and gently applied pressure to an areola, sucking gently. She held his head to her chest, encouraging his exploration as his tongue encircled her and alternating. Kacey matched his desire as she felt herself become damp.

Caleb felt Kacey, and he pushed her lower from the waist and raised her up to enter her slowly. Kacey raised on her knees and fell hard upon him, sheathing only a part of him. Caleb, eager to become one with her again, thrust upward and buried himself a little deeper. He moved for further entry only to find himself restricted by her, and an escaped moan came from his frustration. She smiled, loving his reaction; she met him moving to remove his restrictive position as he guided himself deeper into her warmth as her motion matched his need.

They paused to explore each other, and she gently rocked, stroking him in a back-and-forth motion as he moved upward, filling her. They both enjoyed each other's warmth and ridged contours. Caleb held Kacey as she sat in his lap, facing each other. They were fully connected as one.

Caleb held her bottom and raised her, slowly moving her to a pace, stroking his desire and playfully teasing her to a partial stroke. Kacey cried out with every full inward thrust given intermittently in their action. She wanted more, and he played with her more. Stopping their motion and restricting her, Caleb held her around the waist. He kissed her, letting her feel him growing and pulsating within. She whimpered as his arousal grew; she felt him, unlike the first time.

Her eyes widened as he smiled, knowing she was beginning to understand him. Letting the arousal build, he filled her, and with an upward small thrust, he sheathed within her all she could take. He released his restriction, and she rhythmically stroked his need, possessing all of him in the intimate connection. Caleb turned her and continued his own personal motion with her positioned beneath him in face-to-face missionary. Taking his time, he slowed the pace and grinded her slowly into multiple released orgasms until he heard her again say the words he wanted to hear, and he kissed her to keep the repeated words buried in her throat.

His tongue explored the inner aspects of her mouth. She quivered beneath him as his tongue invaded her, stifling her moans. He pushed his arousal further into her warmth, and she screamed out his name as he released his kiss. His hardened member thrust into her repeatedly without restraint for a moment.

Loving the feel and reaction of her, he continued until he slowed his pace; his last thrust became a deep grind. Keeping her immobile. He unleashed his pent-up want of her, pinning her with short, deep strokes and a rhythmic grind until she began to quiver beneath him. Grabbing her legs, he raised them beyond his waist level, and he kissed the back of each knee, gaining better access. Kacey felt every stroke Caleb gave deep into her until her legs quivered hard, and she climaxed on a hard, fast-paced thrust. Caleb turned her over and kissed the back of her neck.

Kacey never experienced the patience of Caleb, a man seasoned in lovemaking, to hold himself in check. Sprawled upon her, he kissed her as she looked back at him, and he kneed her legs open to a widened V. He entered her from the back missionary style. She cried out as he found other pleasure points within the entrance of her. He tantalized her as he repositioned himself to reach around her, and he finger stroked her at the meeting of her *why...* while repeatedly becoming one with her.

Kacey called out, and Caleb relished in her, enjoying her. Caleb turned them over. Now, on his back, his hands roamed over her body while still being fully sheathed within her. Kacey leaned forward as he looked at her back and watched her ride him. Kacey held his calves as she leaned forward for better mobility, and He held her bottom, increasing her motion.

Caleb let himself go with her dominance. He pushed into her, driving them both over the edge. He gutturally said her name as he let go, releasing within her deep with a satisfaction that was beyond what he thought would be impossible with Kacey. Caleb lay watching his wife sleep. In all his years, he had never experienced such a deep connection, and it surprised him. He thought God is good and all the time God is good...

Newly married, Caleb was enjoying life, but he still held himself in check as his affliction still chased him internally.

Caleb looked out into the church. His wife sitting on the front pew. And he watched the woman get up and walk away. He knew that walk that sway. Caleb woke up from his dream.

Caleb looked around at his home. Kacey had gone off to work, and his flesh was calling for more than what she was able to give with her work schedule. He found himself calling Bethany; his mind began to wander as he thought of times past, and his memories of Bethany began to surface.

He knew he was wrong. His mother's words continued to scream at him. He knew he had to finally face his inner stronghold. He knew most people had thought Kacey and him were in an exclusive relationship with all the travels and trips, before he got married. He even told Bethany- out of spite to make her mad and jealous. He wanted her to feel the pain he felt with her ongoing men he had to hear about. He wanted her to feel the rejection he felt with her inability to be what he needed.

Caleb wanted to make her pay for the pain he felt. Bethany could hate him, but he didn't care. He was mad at the world, and Kacey was his saving grace. But his inner pain needed an outlet. Bethany, while Caleb professed his love and attention, was an antidote, a pacifier to his past pain.

He began to realize she was an obsession that made Reese's words become clear. He was the bad guy trying to live righteously while coping and interacting with past baggage. He wanted Bethany, and in his warped thinking, he loved her.

He thought of Tonya as he heard his mother's voice. He knew he had to repent before God because of his actions. He knew he would suffer for his infidelity. He had to let go and Let God unseal the final issue of his soul's damnation to hell with adultery in his spirit and the lustful desire for something that was not his. So, he thought of Bethany, wanting to finally do right by her. He needed to clear his conscience and tell her the truth. He owed her that much. His actions, less than righteous, weighed heavily upon him. His flesh was weak. He picked up his phone and opened his messenger app.

Bethany heard a bing on her phone after talking with a friend. She looked at the text and questioned What now?

Kacey looked at her phone call during her meeting and knew she needed to be home. Caleb had called more than 6 six times straight. Kacey left her office, trying to reach Caleb. She hated it when he got like this, and she drove straight home. Opening the door to their home, Kacey found Caleb asleep on the sofa. She saw the bottle of liquor. She thought of her father-in-law on days like this. She walked toward him only to see his phone lit and the message to Bethany. She sighed and asked for wisdom and patience as she leaned toward her husband. Inwardly, she knew he fought to keep his inner turmoil at bay. Knowing his heart and feeling his pain, she leaned over and kissed him lightly, awakening him. He reached out for her and held her, his Kacey. She reached and found him wanting. He looked into her eyes.

"You're home."

"I love you, Caleb. Sorry for my long days. I'm here for you."

He looked at her, searching. Finding her eyes full of concern and love unwavering. He reached up and kissed her, breaking the connection; he whispered in her ear as he nibbled on her neck ...

"You know I love you, Kacey?"

Kacey felt he was going to talk, but not wanting to hear his thoughts, she leaned back, found his lips, and deepened the kiss. Her hands trailed and undid his belt buckle to the buttons of his pants and commenced to unzip Caleb's trousers.

Caleb wrapped his arms around her waist as she lifted her skirt. She freed him, holding him in her hand; she stroked him to a moan. He reached around her and pulled away her barrier as she raised a leg to straddle him. Kacey held him and guided him into the place that would quench his desire. Caleb felt her embrace and all that she was willing to give as she rode him into ecstasy.

Bethany checked her phone, thinking about the date and time...God, I need you.

15

COMING TO TERMS

He had no right to want her. He knew he was wrong, wanting his present life and yet clinging to the past. Bethany was no longer his to claim. He made a vow before God and sealed it with marriage. And yet his inner demon clung to his thoughts. His fleshly desires whispered *she could still be yours.*

His flesh called to him as his eyes were drawn to her. He caught a glimpse of the contours of her shape as she walked toward him. Her clothing clung to her in all the right places, and she swayed as she moved. In summary, the demon harassed his inner peace ...

What was I thinking...

Caleb watched her as she walked into his life once again.

Oh my -fine, yes! But beyond that, she challenged me. Provoked me, made me see sides of myself I wanted to keep buried 6 feet under and then some...Why, in my weakest moments, do I call on her?

He felt the stirring in his loins until he really looked at her and listened to her. She was not the same Bethany. The demon within laughed at him, reminding him of his mother's words. LEAVE HER ALONE, but he only heard his inner fear... *too late -too late.*

Caleb let the negative words bombard his mind. His flesh and his emotional thoughts got the best of him. He finally let it wash over him, and a spiritual nudge came to give him hope...

God's Spirit: You got a good woman at home

Caleb: But she is not who I want. Something about that mocha brown, Bethany. She calls me compelling and alluring; she is my forbidden fruit.

God's Spirit: I know the plans I have for you as I have for her....

Caleb: If only I could face my fears. If only I could get out of my own head, maybe, just maybe, I could find peace of mind.

God's Spirit: I can only give you what you are willing to receive.

Caleb: I need you...

God's spirit: I need you to hear me, Caleb. As I wanted to commune with Adam I want to commune with you. Accept me.

Caleb watched Bethany. She walked away again. God help me, she walked away.

Caleb sat looking at the door, and he questioned his motives and thought...

They say men don't pray... I hear you, GOD.

Caleb let his anguish overcome him, the part of his being he didn't want to own up to. The pent-up pain of not wanting to let go. He knew she was not his even though his flesh called to him. He put it into perspective. His trials were still to be... But he had to become the man that GOD ordained. Lukewarm had no place in his true purpose. He picked up his phone and called his wife.

"We need to talk."

Kacey heard it in his voice. The dam had finally broken. "Do you need me to come to you? Better yet, Caleb. Don't drive. Where are you?"

Caleb looked at the phone as Kacey hung up and was on her way. Caleb knew God had him, but he had to believe in GOD.

⸺❤⸺

Caleb's wife, Kacey Mitchell, walked into the establishment. A successful accountant who was deeply in love with Minister Caleb Mitchell, but Caleb was finding it hard to be in love with her fully. Having no spiritual foundation before dating Caleb, Kacey's faith grew. Her personal relationship with God, which kept her grounded and wise in knowing, kept her in times like these.

Caleb watched her as she walked through the very doors that his fleshly desires walked out of...He looked harder as a thought came to mind...

God's Spirit: Whoso findeth a wife findeth a good thing, and obtaineth favour of the LORD.

Kacey looked at Caleb, saying nothing; she walked up to him, took his hand, and said let's go home. Caleb nodded and walked out, head held high as she walked beside him, holding him up. No questions were asked, just giving what he needed in his moment of weakness. He looked at her. *I don't deserve her.* He thought of Tonya and his mother's words: *You have become...*

Kacey opened the passenger door to the vehicle, and Caleb got in, grateful for the dark tint. As he got in on the passenger side and closed the door, Caleb, the man, for the first time since he lost his wife, children, and everything he had worked so hard for, cried for his loss. Caleb had let go in small ways, searching for peace in certain aspects of his life. He looked at Kacey, and he cried because of his infidelity to the woman beside him. Caleb accepted that...He had become what broke him. He observed his wife sitting, waiting... not to condemn him but comforting him quietly. Not agreeing to his mess but quiet in her stance. Giving him space to find his way.

"I'm so sorry, Kacey."

She put her finger to his lips. "Take it up with GOD, Caleb. I know more than you think. Take it up with God. Okay? PLEASE do that for me... Love covers."

Caleb looked at her...thinking... *I love my wife, and we are really good friends. But I was never in love with her.* Then Caleb thought about the word love and what it meant. His flesh was ruling his thoughts of love. However, what she offered to him was beyond the flesh.

Not the younger love... of your yesterday's Caleb... the spirit of God spoke.

Caleb dropped his head back on the seat as Kacey entered into traffic. He kept looking at her, giving side way glances as she concentrated on the busy traffic. *I love her. I really do. She has been absolutely wonderful to me, but I can't continue to be dishonest with her,* he thought to himself. But he remembered her words. Then he thought of the word Love again... He thought of her vows to him. He found it odd when they married the choice of her vows. Different than he could have imagined. But at this moment, he understood what she meant....

She was so secretive of her vows. Caleb had watched her talk in hush tones with his father at times, and he wondered what they were up to... But Caleb would never forget her vows, the very vows that burned into his mind with every indiscretion and action that she did not deserve from him. The very actions and thoughts of Tonya.... He swallowed the lump in his throat. He replayed the vows in his mind... as he looked at her, and she turned toward him for a moment, smiling, asking what? Nothing he said as he looked at her with admiration...And remembered their wedding day.

Kacey stood before him in all her Godly glory, which was beautiful and radiant. Her daughters served as her maid of honor, and the wedding was small. But the highlight was Kacey's words; she cried as she spoke from her heart.

"All my life, I have strived to be the Proverbs 31 woman, even when I didn't know what a Proverbs 31 woman was. But as I have come to gain a better understanding of it since meeting you. By God's word, I will live.

Love is patient, and love is kind. It does not envy, it does not boast, and it is not proud. It is not rude, it is not self-seeking, it is not easily angered, and it keeps no record of wrongs. Love does not delight in evil but rejoices with the truth. I will ask you as we grow together...Caleb, did you find me to be a virtuous woman? Will you see me as that woman whose price is far above rubies? Caleb, I want to be that woman... where your heart doth safely trust, so you have no need of spoil... I will seek God in all his righteousness.

Remembering Proverbs 24, knowing we all fall short and will need God to keep us, I pray you understand what I am offering. As Eve failed with Adam. May GOD order my steps that I keep his statutes...I pray to continue in my way as

Proverb 31:12 To do you good and not evil all the days of my life. As God sees the heart. I will always look at your heart, Caleb. Asking God to give me sight beyond sight to know you...Loving you unconditionally. Not to enable you but to hold you accountable.

But I want to give you the space to be the man God ordained, as you do right by me in your actions to the best of what you can in the midst of all that you have endured and still must endure. I will be here for you.... and we will endure together until you say you wish to put asunder what I know GOD has joined together or until death do us part.

My heart leans towards the latter. I stand before God, giving this vow not taken lightly. Remember my words on your worst of days. During the most tempting moments of your life, so that you find strength. Remember my vow: When you need the most in a world that appears to have forsaken you, and you think you're at your lowest. Remember, God is your head. and I got your back... the gates of hell can't prevail against us... GOD IS IN CONTROL If we let him."

Caleb was outdone with the vows. He cried, telling God I don't deserve her. Kacey made it worth his while, and God whispered. *I know the plans I have for you...*

16

BECOMING AWARE

2 Years Later

Who in the world throws a wedding on Iron Bowl Saturday. I can't believe that she is dragging me to her boss's wedding. She knows that I am a die-hard Auburn fan. I swear I am starting to think that she lied to me about being into sports. I thought our Saturdays would consist of eating wings, drinking beer, and watching college football. All she wants to do is be on every Atlanta social scene. I swear everything has changed since we got married. She doesn't exercise anymore and has gained so much weight. She doesn't watch sports with me, and we barely have sex.

Caleb was disgruntled by his thoughts of how women sometimes present a false picture to secure a man and stop doing those things once they get the man. He absolutely loved

Kacey and was grateful for her commitment to him. Still, one could only imagine if that was enough to keep him happy. All his life Caleb witnessed his dad honoring the vows made to his mother. He remained faithful when her words would have sent any sane man running for the hills. He always wondered if the root of his father's fidelity was love or if he was just honoring his vows to have and to hold his wife from that day forward, for better or worse, for richer or poorer, in sickness and in health, to love and to cherish, *until death....part.*

Is it possible to have the whole package? Kacey was the female version of his father, and maybe that is what was most attractive to him, but he was more of a self-fulfilling prophecy in his mother's words. Caleb had mastered the persona of being fully present. Still, his mind was clearly on the plains of Jordan-Hare Stadium. He rested at the venue bar while Kacey mixed and mingled with other wedding guests. The reception site didn't have a TV, but that didn't stop him from pulling it up on his phone. Through the cheers and the chant, he heard a recognizable laugh. *It couldn't be. Nah. It couldn't be.*

Caleb slightly turned his head to the right. His eyes lay upon a five-foot-seven, mocha complexion, size twelve, looking thick, beautiful black woman wearing a dark green one-shoulder, draped split body con dress that stopped right above her knees with beige pumps. Her hair was pulled up into a sleek bun with dangling earrings. It was her, but she was not alone. His heart began to ache as he watched the woman who he truly loved walk hand in hand with this Djimon Hounsou-looking man.

"Hey, babe! The reception is starting soon. Let's go inside and take our seats."

Kacey had startled him as if he had just been caught cheating. Bigger thoughts now roamed his mind as he watched Bethany being escorted like the queen she was to her seat.

Damn, God forgive me… Did her ass get bigger? Not ass, …but, dang-shoot, that dress is fitting her like a glove. Caleb couldn't help but notice that Bethany appeared to be in the best shape of her life. She never wore that type of dress with him. Not that Bethany didn't look good in her athletic wear, but that was her almost daily wear. *How come she is dressing up for him? Is he the reason she walked away from me?*

Caleb's thoughts could have added another verse to Drake's *Hotline Bling* lyrics. The wonders of what she was doing for this man caused him to be envious, but his poker face hid the anguish that his heart was feeling. At this moment, he realized that time would never eliminate the love he had for Bethany. Much like the love he had for his mother, he knew without a shadow of a doubt that, by observing Bethany's happiness, he would have to learn to live without it.

"Earth to Caleb." Kacey sang, trying to snap him out of his daze.

"Yeah, my bad babe."

"Are you okay?"

"Yeah, I'm good."

"Look, I know that you don't really want to be here."

Caleb looked at Kacey and then across the room. His eyes took on a dazed look as he thought. *If she only knew how the tables had turned. Thankfully, Kacey doesn't know that I absolutely want to be here now that Bethany has arrived.* Acknowledging,

Caleb looked back at Kacey. "No, it's cool. I got to catch some of the highlights of the game," Caleb said calmly, concealing his true emotions and thoughts.

"I really appreciate you doing this for me," Kacey said as she leaned forward to give him a kiss on the cheek.

As they entered the reception hall, Caleb's eyes automatically found Bethany as Asa leaned in and gave her the softest kiss upon her clear mocha skin. They shared food off of each other's plates. His heart mourned internally as he watched them begin to dance to New Edition's *If It Isn't Love.*

He had discovered both of their love for New Edition on their first date at the park in downtown Huntsville. This was the same day that he realized that Bethany was 100 percent of the woman that he desired. Even though she was more than a decade younger than him, Bethany had an old soul. Her biblical intellect spoke to his spirit, and her physique spoke to his flesh. Her pleasure for sports matched the sports fanatic that he was. Unlike Tonya, Bethany came from a two-parent home like himself. She had a good relationship with her dad, as he had with his father. He knew that a woman with a solid relationship with her father could help avoid getting with a woman with daddy issues.

That is supposed to be me dancing with her, Caleb thought before Kacey rudely interrupted his trip down memory lane. "That's a beautiful, fun couple." Kacey smilingly said. "She's gorgeous too. I love that dress on her."

Bethany and Asa had the spotlight on the dance floor as they performed similar dance moves from the 80's and 90's. Even the bride and the groom cheered them on and hyped up their moves. The beats inside Caleb's chest internally echoed the words of Fred Samford. *This was the big one.*

Kacey was admiring Bethany now, but what if she knew it was Bethany-Bethany. Kacey was well aware that Caleb was once madly in love with Bethany and the many reasons why. Even though Bethany was an ex, she could tell from how he talked about her that he still loved her. During the development of their relationship, Kacey knew that in order to seal the deal with Caleb, she had to be everything Bethany was to him and give him the one thing she did not...blind loyalty.

She didn't concern herself with his past financial hardships. Kacey took care of her man and supported him through the death of his father and his own health scares. She wanted him to know that she was not like Tonya or Bethany or any other woman who might run at the first sight of hardship. Even when she got suspicious of the late nights of him hanging out with so-called friends, she never questioned his faithfulness.

After years of being in an established career and financially stable yet being alone, she was determined to make this marriage work and be the submissive wife that she believed God wanted her to be. Besides, she believed it was the nature of a man to cheat. She just better not find out about it and have it invade her world personally.

Caleb made significantly less than her, but she respected

the values of being a Christian wife and submitted to him as the head of her house. She accepted the fact that her money could not fill the emptiness that only a man could fill in her life as ordained by her Creator.

Fearful of the anticipated interaction that he knew would occur before the night ended, Caleb imagined the lid of his adulterous secrets twisting off. He contemplated how to get Bethany's attention for a private conversation. Maybe he could convince her to pretend as if they do not know one another. He quickly erased that thought because he knew any close contact with Bethany would make it harder to hide the erection he would get from the lust to kiss and touch her one more time.

Hand in hand, Bethany and Asa began to walk back to their seats, stopping to acknowledge the fans that they just made off their performance. Getting closer and closer to Caleb's table, he contemplated telling Kacey who that woman was. His tongue was stuck to the roof of his mouth as the couple stopped directly in front of him.

"Oh my God! Hi Caleb. How are you?"

Bethany said. In his silence, Bethany turned to Asa. "Babe, this is Caleb."

"So, you are Caleb," Asa said while extending his hand with a confirmation that Caleb was no threat to his relationship with Bethany, "I have heard a lot about you."

Caleb stood, hoping that his insecurity could not be detected as he began to size Asa up. He knew Bethany liked her men chocolate and tall, but he never knew she liked them black on black. He could smell the Acqua Di Gio scent that matched his perfectly tailored Armani suit. Despite how small he felt to this Mandingo-looking warrior and the dough that he must have been rolling in, Caleb stood confidently and gave Asa a firm handshake.

In an octave-lower voice, Caleb managed to tell Asa not to believe everything he had heard. "Oh, I believe everything that comes from this angel's lips," Asa replied as he slid his hand to the small of Bethany's back. Shrinking smaller than a microscopic cell inside, Caleb tried to regain control of the moment even though he was feeling a lot of regret.

How could I have let this beautiful, spiritually successful woman go?

He began to think about his personal insecurities and family trauma that would not allow him to fully embrace Bethany after their multiple breakups. He regretted that he had not been the type of person that he desired in a mate. He did not give Bethany blind loyalty, but he definitely expected it. Caleb began to realize that his acceptance issues had nothing to do with Bethany. It began in his mother's womb. At this moment, he realized that these issues had caused him to lose the woman his heart would always love, but he decided that now was the perfect time to hype up the woman that his heart trusted.

"Forgive my manners." Caleb reached down and grabbed

Kacey's hand to assist her. "Kacey, this is Bethany." Pulling Kacey closer to him, he continued as he began to turn his head to look her in her eyes, "Bethany, this is my beautiful, smart, intelligent best friend. My wife...Kacey." Kacey did not let her inner insecurities get the best of her. Holding her ground even though she was at a loss, she rethought her compliments.

How was I to know? I had no earthly idea; I had verbally admired the woman who still may have Caleb's heart. I wondered if this was the reason he had felt so distant just moments ago. I knew he was a football fanatic, but my God, he even sat at this table listening to my compliments about his ex, and he did not say a word until now. What's this all about!?!

She observed answering her own questions and prayed to God at the same time. As her near-sighted and far-sighted vision collided, she pretended not to be slightly jealous, being honest with herself. She gained 20-20 clarity of just how amazing Bethany appeared to be with her perfect waist, beautiful mocha skin, and fun personality. Her 20-20 vision brought her personal ownership of how she had let her own weight get out of control as she chose frequent eat-out bonding moves to keep the feel-good moments over continuing her premarital dieting and exercising habits. She had no one to blame for her appearance but herself.

Kacey looked at Bethany and refused to hate another black woman. She knew from Caleb that Bethany was not always this size either. Still, this sista girl has truly done the work, and Kacey took note to use her as motivation to get her sexy back.

Kacey did not see a ring on Bethany's finger. However,

it was self-evident that Bethany was madly in love with Asa, which eased her thoughts of Bethany still wanting Caleb. Either way, Kacey felt a moment of victory because when it came to Caleb, she was the one who God had chosen.

17

⧽◈⧼

CALEB'S LIFE

With a victorious smile, Kacey extended her right hand and greeted Bethany with, "It is so nice to finally meet you."

Bethany smiled an open, honest smile. Knowing Kacey's loyalty, she genuinely stated the same. Both women knew that God had made the spiritual connection that could only occur with God in the midst–each gave respect and prayed for each other's well-being as God ordained....

Caleb watched Asa as Asa sized him up. Both brothers watched their women meet but were silently in a mental battle. Asa's inner spirit quenched his worldly thoughts. He silently prayed as he recognized Caleb for the second time in his life.

This is Minister Mitchell? This is the man Bethany had to spiritually fast and pray about to relinquish soul ties to accept me? The same Minister Caleb Mitchell who stood in the pulpit only to walk down from it during a sermon and became raw and open to the brothers in the church?

Asa remembered the day... it was his take me back to when I first believed moment with God. His first time understanding, *I don't have to have it all together; I just have to be willing to live righteous point forward.* Minister Mitchell spoke it plain, and Asa remembered the sermon words....

You will be tempted. You will fall sometimes. HEAVEN KNOWS I have. But it is the grace and the heart to want to do and seek to do what's right. You will have temptations that will be God's project. Some you may never overcome. But God knows ...

Asa stood with all this in his mind as he looked at Caleb. Caleb watched Asa, but his mind settled on Bethany. She was more of what he saw as she left him at the bookstore. She was free. Her eyes and demeanor let him know his time had come and gone. To approach her unrighteously would be met with the mindset of his father now Resting in Peace. Godliness and unrighteousness are unequally yoked. Bethany had moved on.

His attention moved to seeing Asa for the first time, letting go of any opposition except loss, and hearing the title minister, which stirred up a feeling in Kacey.

Yes, for such a time as this, Proverb 31 becomes a reality, Kacey thought as she and Bethany spoke briefly about it as they watched the men. Only to hear the word, Minister.

Asa spoke... "Minister Mitchell," as he looked at Bethany

and then Caleb. "God is interesting. HIS thoughts are not our thoughts, nor his ways are our ways, but I am grateful."

Caleb felt a spiritual nudge to leave his fleshly thoughts. *Cling unto me, my son.* The Spirit of GOD beckoned him to return his thoughts to HIM. Caleb's calling in life, his purpose in life, compelled him to let go and let God. HE heard the word minister, and he recognized God in Asa, and they connected God's spirit to God's spirit. Caleb listened. *For when two or three are gathered in my name, there shall I BE...*

"Minister Mitchell, I remember you speaking at the men's retreat years ago. Because of your testimony, I let go and let God. Never had I heard a man speak so plainly so openly about his struggles in life. Some ministers want people to worship the ground they walk on while you know they are sleeping around, while others are money-hungry and are not living the life they preach about. YOU on that night, I saw you as you walked down from the pulpit, sat at the altar, and spoke to us men directly. Then you turned your back to us and cried out to God for your sins."

Caleb nodded in remembrance as Asa continued.

"The ministers in the pulpit some found redemption, and others as I watched held firm... so many men gave their lives to God that night, and you were oblivious to it all as another minister had to take over as you cried out. Something women don't get to truly see a man after God's heart. We hold it in until we feel comfortable."

Bethany looked at Asa with so much love it wasn't lost on Caleb and Kacey. Caleb watched as Asa and Bethany walked away, and he turned to look at Kacey. He thought of his mother and all the women who were in his life. He remembered his mother calling what was yet to come with his infidelity as she lay in the hospital bed, and then he thought of his youth.

He looked at Kacey and saw his father as he finally could acknowledge his own brokenness in his life clearly with Asa's story. A scripture boldly forced its way through Caleb's thoughts: Jeremiah 29:11. The very scripture his mother kept on her nightstand. And Caleb's dam broke free... the thoughts he had forgotten. The ones that made him realize why he married Tonya and the pain of losing his first child due to culture and the ocean of separation. He remembered his mother, and he saw more of what he had buried in pain. Pictures flooded his mind. JEREMIAH 29:11.

His mother prayed that prayer with him nightly. He remembered the slight kiss upon his forehead, the gentle smile when no one was watching that he'd see before she turned away. His mother loved him. His thoughts lingered on Bethany. Why her? What held him to Bethany.... And it all became clear... Bethany was safe. She didn't ask beyond what he could give. She accepted. It was only in those moments of non-acceptance that he and Bethany found an issue with each other.

As with Tonya, she pushed him but didn't support him. Kacey pushed him and held him. She required him to be a man. Kacey held her standards and expected him to be and to do more. She fussed and laid the foundation that support never faltered. Bethany was Caleb's sanctuary, a safe space where he could find comfort. Yet, her love unintentionally stirred up his lingering emotional wounds from childhood. As with Tonya, Bethany did not demand that he confront or heal these wounds. She pushed but did not support. On the other hand, Kacey's love was a healing force for Caleb. She recognized his pain and vulnerability, offering a nurturing and supportive love that facilitated his emotional healing.

Kacey's unconditional love provided a protective shield of grace around Caleb, creating a steadfast foundation of unwavering support that never wavered. Kacey gave him unconditional love as God intended. She held him to a high regard, and while doing so... she saw him in all his glory when no one else did, faults and all. Caleb just had to see it for himself; he had to do what he preached to others. Let go and let God...

Caleb brought Kacey closer to his side with a one-arm embrace. He kissed her temple ever so lovingly and whispered thank you. Kacey looked up at him, tears glistening. She mouthed I love you.

He looked at her, staring longingly. Then, he leaned down and kissed her softly...and he let his flesh get the best of him as he wanted to leave the social event, which made Kacey smile knowingly and securely... for she saw for the first time her husband only had eyes for his wife--- and she with God would continue loving Caleb.

ABOUT THE AUTHOR

Sandreka Brown, a proud Alabama native now living in Atlanta, is a storyteller with a deep passion for exploring the intricacies of love and life with empathy and insight. Her literary journey began with the debut of, *Love Bethany*, followed by the touching story of *The Birds and The Bees*. Sandreka has also penned inspirational works such as *Teacher to Teacher* and *The Teacher's Keeper*, devotionals created to uplift and support educators, along with the *Dear God* prayer writing journal.

With her third novel, *Loving Caleb*, Sandreka continues to captivate readers with her compelling storytelling and deep emotional insights. Her work reflects a unique blend of grace and authenticity, drawing from life, love, and faith. When she's not writing, Sandreka enjoys exploring the vibrant culture of Atlanta and cherishing time with her loved ones.